THE WALL

A horrifying true story of a haunting

by
Cindy Sarro

Bloomington, IN  Milton Keynes, UK

AuthorHouse™
1663 Liberty Drive, Suite 200
Bloomington, IN 47403
www.authorhouse.com
Phone: 1-800-839-8640

AuthorHouse™ UK Ltd.
500 Avebury Boulevard
Central Milton Keynes, MK9 2BE
www.authorhouse.co.uk
Phone: 08001974150

This book is a work of non-fiction. Unless otherwise noted, the author and the publisher make no explicit guarantees as to the accuracy of the information contained in this book and in some cases, names of people and places have been altered to protect their privacy.

© *2006 Cindy Sarro. All rights reserved.*

No part of this book may be reproduced, stored in a retrieval system, or transmitted by any means without the written permission of the author.

First published by AuthorHouse 2/16/2006

ISBN: 1-4208-8037-3 (sc)

Printed in the United States of America
Bloomington, Indiana

This book is dedicated to my Grandmother Lucille Raymer and my loving mother Anita Sarro. This book would have never been written if not for my mother. Thank you mom for all the encouragement. I also want to thank all of my family and friends for believing in me and standing by me through one of the worst experiences in my life.

I would like to tell you a little bit about myself before you read my story. My name is Cindy. I have a sister that is three years older than myself, her name is Taylor. I have lived in Caseyville, Illinois most of my life. My parents divorced when I was still a baby. My mother remarried when I was around four years old. By the time I was eight, my stepfather was murdered outside of our home. I couldn't understand why he had to die. I cried a lot and asked God why? One day I was lying on the couch with my eyes closed and I asked God if my stepfather was ok. I asked if he was in heaven, to let me know somehow. At that moment, I felt someone squeeze my hand real tight. I opened my eyes but no one was there. I had communicated with the other side and it scared me. After that day, strange things started happening to me. I always felt as if someone was watching me. Although I couldn't see anyone, I would always feel their presence. Then when I would lie down to go to sleep, I would leave my body. I was afraid because I always thought I was dying. Years later, I found out a lot of psychics do this and it's called Astral Projection. Many times, I would dream things and they would happen. I also began having weird feelings when my mother was sick or when something bad was going to happen. As I got older, I wouldn't just feel the presence of someone, they would actually appear.

I was very close to an aunt of mine, she was like a second mother to me. Her name was Joy. I always confided everything to her, we could talk about anything. One day she said, "Cindy, you know I won't be here forever." I told her to quit talking like that; she was only forty one years old. We had always talked about death before but it scared me. She said, "Cindy, if I die before you and there really is a heaven, I will come back to let you know."

I said I would do the same if I was the one to go first. I was devastated when I got a call saying my aunt had died. I couldn't believe it. Someone was surely playing a cruel joke on me. When I found out it was true, I just couldn't accept it. I cried and cried. I realized later that she knew she was going to die and she tried to prepare me. I was so mad at her for leaving me. She had always been there for me. She was only forty one years old and she was too young to die. I use to talk to her every day on the telephone and when she died, I would find myself picking up the phone to call her and would realize she was no longer there. One day my daughter Sydney, who had just turned three years old, came running in the room I was in. She had been watching cartoons, and usually when cartoons were on, I had time to myself. Sydney wouldn't budge from the TV. I had been crying thinking about my aunt when Sydney came in the room. She said, "Mommy, Aunt Joy said not to cry. She is happy now, she's not sick anymore." I asked her who had said that. She replied, "Aunt Joy mommy." I said, "Aunt Joy couldn't have told you that." At that moment, Sydney walked out of the room and wanted me to follow. I followed and she took me in the kitchen and told me Aunt Joy was standing in the kitchen .I asked Sydney where she went and she said, "Aunt Joy said she was tired and had to leave now." I knew that Aunt Joy kept her promise to me. She was letting me know there was a heaven and that she is happy. She didn't want me to mourn for her anymore. Joy passed away in 1985. Maybe she didn't want to appear to me because as close as we were, I might not have been able to handle it. Joy never appeared in front of me. Instead, she would come to me in dreams. To this day, she communicates with me that way.

 I have come in contact with a lot of spirits since I was a small child. I was always told this was a gift. I was gifted to be able to see and feel things. I have also been told that I'm like a magnet to spirits, I draw them to me. This gift I have, almost ruined my life. You will find that out when you read my story.

 In October of 1982, I had a freak accident which left my back in bad shape. At the time this happened, my daughter Sydney was only seven months old. I felt bad all of the time, I could hardly lift her. After running back and forth to doctors for years, a specialist had me hospitalized over in St. Louis, Mo. I thought I would have surgery and everything would be fine once again. A well known surgeon was called in. After much testing, the news wasn't what I wanted to hear. He said surgery wasn't possible in my case because I had a ruptured disc in the lower area of my back. If I would have surgery, I would be paralyzed because of where it was located. He said he wouldn't touch it and I wouldn't find another surgeon that would, it was too risky. I had to learn to live with the pain. I would never be able to hold a full time job again.

I had a boyfriend named Jake that I had been dating since Sydney was three months old. I became pregnant with his child and gave birth to another daughter in October of 1983. Jake and I talked about getting married, and then he got laid off his job. We also argued quite frequently so I didnt think marriage was such a good idea. I had severe back trouble for years. A lot of times, my back would go out and I wouldn't be able to walk at all. Since Jake stayed at his parents most of the time, my mom would help out with the girls when she could. She was sick a lot and I didn't want to bother her too much. If I needed help, I knew I could always count on her. My niece Haley helped out also. Jake wasn't much help in the money department, his money was his own.

Around September of 1989, I moved to Belleville, IL. It was a half hour drive from my house to my moms. I was supposed to be getting some money from my back injury. I figured I would buy a house in Caseyville. I finally got my money right before Christmas in late 1990. I kept renting the duplex I had been living in. By then, the children had close friends and they loved the school they were attending in Belleville. By the spring of 1991, I had decided to start looking for a house to buy. After all, what I was paying for rent could have been a house payment. I wanted to start looking in Caseyville. At the time, Jake was living with me and the girls once again. We were getting along better than we ever had. Jake had a fit when I said I was moving back to Caseyville. "Cindy, you will be taking the girls away from their friends, and you know they love the school." He pointed out everything, reasons why I should buy a house in Belleville and not in Caseyville. I finally gave in and started looking for a house in Belleville. I found a few I was interested in. When my mother's boyfriend found out, he called and asked me to reconsider. He said my mom needed me to be closer to her. He was right, I missed not being able to see my mom every day like I use to. Besides, Belleville was long distance to call her so my phone bills were getting high. My mom needed me and I knew that. I discussed it with Jake. He wasn't very happy about it but he finally agreed. The girls weren't disappointed at all, they still had friends back in Caseyville. It wasn't like they couldn't visit their friends in Belleville. That's when the dreams started or should I say, terrifying nightmares. I would be running down stairs and someone would be behind me, chasing me. I never could see who it was. I could just feel the fear of someone trying to kill me. The first time I had this dream, I woke up unbelievably scared. It had seemed so real to me. I looked around the house and the only stairs we had were the ones in the basement and looked nothing like the ones in my dream. I pushed the dream out of my mind as I got caught up in the excitement of finding my own house. The excitement was soon shortlived. I had the dream once again and this time it really bothered me. I knew though, I had a lot of things to do and couldn't sit around worrying about some dream. I had been looking in the paper for a house and I still hadn't found one. The reoccurring nightmare had seemed to slip into my dreams for a third time, and this time I was really upset.

    I got up and got the girls off to school and headed for my mom's house. I was almost there when a FOR SALE sign caught my eye. It was walking distance to both Jake's parent's house and my mom's house. I stopped the van and found myself staring up at a house on a hill. The house itself, almost seemed to be staring back at me. It was shaped like a barn. I remembered years ago I went to school with some boys who had lived there. Well this house was on a steep hill and I didn't care for hills at all. My mom's house is on a hill and in the winter time, I could never get up it. This hill was a lot steeper than hers. This house was a definite no. I pushed on the gas pedal and drove a block to my mom's house. When I got up her hill, I was happy to see that Haley was there. I went in and began talking. I told them about my reoccurring dream. They both said, "the way you and Jake argue, are you sure it's not him?" They started laughing. I said, "I don't know, I can never see the person." I was trying to be serious. They were both joking about it so I began to laugh too. What the hell, maybe it was Jake, but I had doubts. Before I knew it, it was time for me to get back to Belleville.

    I finally found a house I was interested in. It was right behind the school in Caseyville. To me, it was perfect. The girls could come home every day for lunch. You could see the back of the school from the front door. Jake had spotted the house on the hill. We had been in both houses. Jake was impressed with the barn shaped house. I really don't think it was the house itself, more like the property. After you got up on the hill, there was a trailer on the right side of the house. There was also a circle drive that was full of flowers, it was beautiful. There were flowers all around the house too. In the back yard, there was a hill that led to a lot of land and some woods. You could get to Jake's mom's house through the woods. The kids could walk to my mom's house or Jake's mom's house within five minutes. That all sounded good. It was the house itself that I wasn't so sure of. There was a screened in porch that was full of plants which made the porch look nice. Once inside the house, if you turned to your right, there was a staircase. To the left, was a small TV living room. If you went straight ahead when entering the front door, it led right to the kitchen, which was quite large. To the left of that, were some cafe doors that opened up into the laundry room. There was also a small bathroom off to the right in the laundry room. The first floor was built underground. It was very dark and gloomy. If you went up the staircase, there was a bathroom to the right. Straight ahead was a living room with a fireplace plus two bedrooms. Jake and I began arguing about the two houses. Jake's mom even sided with me and said I would regret it in the winter time. All Jake could think of was all of the property. He would say, "Cindy, we could always build a larger house in the back. With all of that property, we could do a lot." I thought about the way we always separated. Who would be stuck with all of the yard work? It wasn't going to be Jake and it surely wouldn't be me with my back condition. I could handle the yard work at the house by the school because the yard was very small. I even had someone check each house out. I was told that if I was going to buy a house, I should purchase the one behind the school. Even after having someone check the houses out, it wasn't good enough for Jake. It was my money and it should have been my choice. Jake and I began arguing so much that in the end, I gave in. I agreed to buy the house on the hill. By giving into Jake, I made the worst mistake of my life. I not only ruined my life, but also the lives of my children.

I should have known something wasn't right from the start. First the loan wouldn't go through, and then the house had to have a new roof. It was one thing after another. To me, these things were bad omens. I even told Jake I wasn't meant to buy the house. After awhile, the roof was fixed and the loan went through in September of 1991.

Jake hired a few guys he worked with to help us move, so we started moving our things in the house. We were carrying things in, when a small boy came over and introduced himself. He said his name was Brett and he lived in the trailer. Jake told him to come back after everything was moved in. I was glad Brett came over. Sydney was around nine and Lindsey was around seven. Brett looked to be more Lindsey's age. I was thankful they would have someone to play with on this hill. Brett went back to the trailer and we continued moving things in. I don't know how many trips we made but it was late and we decided to call it a day. We still had a lot more to move so we went back to Belleville that night. The guys Jake hired wouldn't be able to make it the next day but my uncle Nick said he would help us.

Jake and I got an early start the next morning. The flowers that I thought were so beautiful, now kept us from entering our new home. There were bees, wasps, and hornets all over. The place was swarming with them. I had never seen so many in my life. I took the girls over to my mom's house. When I got back, me and Jake got some spray to kill the bugs. We got shovels and started digging all of the flowers up. Some of the roots were really tough and it seemed like they went on forever. They were deep in the ground. Since the flowers were surrounding the house, it took hours to get all of them up. We still didn't have our refrigerator moved but we did have a cooler full of soda. When we were finished, we got a soda and started moving more things in the house. Later, we picked the girls up and went back to Belleville to load up again. Eventually we got about everything out of the old house. By the time we took the last load in, we were all hot and exhausted. We decided to wait on moving the refrigerator until the next day. I stood looking around the kitchen at all of the boxes. I was standing there and all at once I had the strangest feeling when I looked at the staircase. I had been so caught up in buying the house and the excitement of moving that I hadn't really paid attention. At that moment, it was like a slap in the face. Those steps were more than just familiar; they were the same steps that were in my dreams.

Jake was off work for a few days but after that, he would be back to work and working nights at that. I wondered if the girls and I would be safe in this house. I was standing there thinking about my dreams when I heard Jake. It was really hot in the house so Jake went to open the windows only to discover most of the downstairs ones were fake. The previous owners had said they replaced all the windows; they didn't bother to tell us they were only for looks. Jake was really mad. As for me, at least I didn't have to worry about me and the girls having someone break in at night. I could lock the screened in porch, plus the front door. What I didn't know at the time, was my nightmare was right inside the house. It was right there watching me, just waiting for the right time to attack me. It was strange, all the times we had come up to the house it was always cool, even on the hottest day. The previous owners said they didn't have central air because they didn't need it. They had one small unit in the upstairs living room which they said cooled the upstairs off pretty good. Right now, it felt like we were in hell! Everyone was hot and sweaty. We all decided to go upstairs and turn on the air to get cooled off. Jake turned it on and all that came out was hot air. We sat and waited to feel the cool air but it never came. I made a mental note to call about getting central air. I told the girls to go ahead and get their baths so they could cool off.

All at once, I heard screaming. I ran to the bathroom to see a black substance in the tub. I took the girls to my moms for a bath. She told me they could spend the night. She tried to talk me into staying also but I declined. I had too much to do. I hated to leave her apartment, it was so cool. I did though and when I got back to the house, I started putting canned goods into the cabinets. When I went to open the cabinet door, it fell off. Then they all began falling off. Jake said not to worry that he could fix them. All of the sudden, the lights began flickering. When they stopped, I put the canned goods in the cabinets and stood the doors up. We plugged the can opener and toaster in and we were left in the dark. Jake checked the circuit and it had blown. When he got the lights back on, they went crazy in the kitchen. I decided to sit down for a minute. My kitchen chairs were the type that had wheels on them. I sat down and took off across the room. The floor wasn't level. "The kids are going to love this", I thought. I could just see us trying to sit down and eat a meal with our chairs going every which way. I went to the room we made into a TV room and put the TV on the stand and it fell forward. I caught it just in time. I looked down at the floor. Unleveled wasn't even the word for it. The floor was raised up so high that it looked like a small hill. Why hadn't I noticed this before? Maybe it was the way the previous owners had their furniture arranged.

Jake said he was going to get a snake from his dad to fix the bathtub upstairs. I decided to go ahead and take a shower downstairs. I began to feel better until I stepped out of the shower. There was a huge puddle of water that covered the entire floor. Aggravated, I went upstairs to brush my teeth. It wasnt long before I realized the sink had stopped up. What was going on around here? I went to turn the bathroom light off. To my surprise, it went back on. I told Jake about it and he said he would get a longer chain. The lights were still going crazy downstairs. I told Jake this was a dump and I didn't know how anybody could live in it. By now, Jake was getting aggravated himself. We were up all night trying to get things in order.

The next morning, the girls were back home. I tried to be cheerful but it was hard to do. My uncle Nick showed up to move the refrigerator, washer, and dryer. He asked me what was wrong. I replied, "Everything". When the refrigerator arrived, I bent down to plug it in and the receptacle went right through the wall. Now I was in tears. I said, "What next?" I should have never asked. We discovered that the utility room wasn't wired for my 210 dryer. Well between getting central air and having the room rewired, it was going to cost me. I called about the central air and it would be another few weeks before the guy could come out. I even tried to use the garbage disposal and it didn't work. I called the real estate agent that sold me the house. I told her everything that had been happening. After a few calls, she finally got in touch with the previous owners. They said they had never had any of those problems. If they didn't, then why me?

Mom was at the house and we were sitting there discussing what was happening. She reminded me that she told me not to buy the house because it was too dark and gloomy. Well it was too late now. Since I had a clothesline outside, I put a load of wash in the washer. When the washer stopped, I put the clothes in the basket and took them outside to hang. I was shocked when I picked the clothes up. They were not what you called dirty to begin with but now they were covered with a black oily substance. I brought the clothes back in the house and sat down and cried. What the hell was going on around here anyway? Now my washer went out so it would have to be replaced. Mom offered to go with me the next day to get a new one. Since it was September, the girls had to get enrolled in school soon. So that was next on my list. Brett's mom came over and introduced herself, her name was Kendra. I liked her right away; she seemed like a very nice person. She told me her boyfriend Bruce lived with her and Brett. She worked at a local bar and said her sister Janet stayed at the trailer a lot because she babysat Brett. I told her Jake was getting ready to go back to work and that he worked nights. She said not to worry because someone was always at the trailer and they could see whoever came up the hill. She said she had never had any trouble since she lived there.

Brett and the girls got to be best buddies. He came over every day to play with the girls while I was still unpacking. Sydney was real excited to start school. Before we had moved to Belleville, she had attended Caseyville School. She was anxious to see her old classmates. I went to enroll the girls and was told the classrooms were already full and they would have to attend a different school. Brett was just as disappointed as the girls were. He would have to go to Caseyville School by himself. The superintendent needed to check things out and decide where the girls would attend school. The girls and I went back home. We had a lot of unpacking to do. So when we got home, I started going through boxes. I had just bought bunk beds for the girls and they arrived.

The girls were in their bedroom putting things in order when Sydney came running out with a strange look on her face. I was busy myself but I stopped and asked her what was wrong. Her only reply was, "I don't want to be in that room." Lindsey wouldn't go in the room without her sister. I continued to do what I was doing with the girls following right behind me. I was getting real disgusted when I heard a knock at the door. Jake had already left for work so the girls ran downstairs to answer the door. It was Kendra and Brett. I talked to Kendra for a few minutes. I told her to leave Brett so he could play with the girls for awhile. Since the girls wouldn't play in the bedroom, Brett helped move the boxes of toys into the living room upstairs. I didn't want all of those toys in the living room so I suggested we all carry the toys downstairs. The utility room was big enough to make a toy room on one side. Ever since the girls were old enough to play with toys, they always had a toy room so it worked out perfectly. I still had a lot of things to unpack so I started going through some of the boxes on the top floor. The children were busy playing when I noticed the lights in the utility room were going from bright to almost nothing. I said something to the kids about it and they said the lights had been doing that since they started playing. I blew a lot of light bulbs that night.

I told Brett it was time for him to go home and the girls were going to get their bath and get ready for bed. I had the girls all ready for bed when Sydney said, "mom please don't make me sleep in that room." I asked, "Why, what's wrong?" "I don't like it either" Lindsey agreed. I wasn't too thrilled about them sleeping in my bedroom either. There was something about my closet that gave me the creeps. So I said, "Since daddy isn't here at night anyway, you two can sleep in our bed and I will sleep on the couch." I tucked them in bed and kissed them goodnight. I went back in the living room and sat on the couch. I looked around the room and it was beginning to look really nice. My eyes stopped at the fireplace. I got that weird feeling again. I already told Jake not to light it. When he asked why, I just said, "Don't light it." I know that sounds strange but it was as if someone had told me. I watched TV for awhile when I felt my eyes closing. I was sound asleep when something woke me up. My eyes went straight to the wall that led into my children's room. They were in my bedroom but I got an erie feeling that someone was in their room watching me. I had the TV on plus two lamps in the living room. I have always slept with the lights on since I had come in contact with spirits. Some that were not too nice, may I add. I had always slept with lights on ever since I was pregnant with Sydney and saw scary things. I noticed there was a talk show on when I was awakened, one that I had never seen on before. I checked all the rooms upstairs and downstairs but everything checked out fine. I sat on the couch and started watching the talk show when my eyes went back to the wall. I noticed my heart started skipping beats.

The next morning, I told Jake about the lights going dim and all of the bulbs I was blowing. We both agreed that it was time to call an electrician out. I took the girls to their new school and neither of them were pleased with it. They would still be riding the bus with Brett but they would be going to different schools. I came back home and unpacked some more things. I didn't get much sleep the night before and decided to lie down on the couch for a few minutes. I closed my eyes and the next thing I knew, I was out of my body. I didn't leave the house. All of the sudden, I was being hit in the stomach and in the lower back. The pain was unbearable. I couldn't see who was doing it but I felt it. After each blow, I pleaded in my mind, "please stop, it hurts, leave me alone!" Then I asked God to help me. "Please, God make it stop!" all at once, I was back in my body. I opened my eyes and sat up. I couldn't believe what had just happened. I had been leaving my body since I was eight years old. That's almost twenty six years ago and nothing like this has ever happened to me before. Shaken, I picked up the phone and called my best friend, who is my mother. Since she knew everything about me, maybe she would know why this was happening. I explained everything to her but she said, "Cindy, you moved a lot of things today and you know you have been overdoing it lately. It probably just felt like someone was hitting you." I agreed with her but when I hung the phone up, I knew better. My mom always gave me good advice and I could always go to her with a question and she always had the right answer. This time she was wrong and I knew it. I was beat by something real strong. I didn't understand it myself but I know what I felt. The pain was unlike anything I had ever felt before and it wasn't something I had just imagined. I got up off the couch, I needed to get myself together before the kids got home from school. All of the sudden the TV in the kid's room started blaring. Jake was in our bedroom asleep and I was the only one in the house. I went in and turned the TV off.

    The electrician was due out in a few days. I was still blowing bulbs like crazy and the circuit kept kicking off. The next few nights were the same, the girls would play with Brett in the utility room and the lights would keep dimming. I would give the girls their bath and when they were through, I would pull the chain to turn the light off and it would come back on. Jake added a longer chain but it didn't help. It would still come back on. I would tuck the girls in bed every night then go lay down on the couch. The same thing would happen, I would doze off only to be awakened. Each night before I went to sleep, I would pray for God to be with us and for me not to leave my body. I still didn't know who or what was waking me up. Since my eyes were always fixed to the wall, I was sure it had something to do with it. Also the talk show was just starting every time I was awakened. I knew it was the same time every night. I was so glad to see the electrician the next morning. Lately the girls' TV was coming on more often. Jake was awake one day and he heard it come on by itself. The electrician began checking everything out. My uncle Timmy came over when the electrician was there. That was one thing I liked about being back in Caseyville, my mom came from a large family and most of them lived here so I always had relatives around. The electrician was outside for awhile when he came in and said something about wires that were underground. He went into the TV room where the circuit box was located. When he came back he said, "Folks, I hate to tell you this but someone purposely turned your wiring around." How could that be? Jake and I were the only ones in the house and we didn't do it. The electrician fixed the wires in the box. When he was getting ready to leave, he asked me if anything else was wrong. I said, "Yes, the TV in my children's room keeps going on by itself." I remember my uncle and the electrician having a weird look on their faces but no one said a word. The electrician said if I had anymore problems, to give him a call. My uncle left right after him. That night, everything seemed alright with the electricity but as always, I was awakened.

I was getting around two hours of sleep every night. I would sit up and stare at the wall. The man finally came out and put the central air unit in. It cost me close to two thousand dollars. When I turned the unit on though, it was worth the money. Everybody said it was stupid now because it was getting cooler. I told everybody that at least I wouldn't have to wait until next summer. What I didn't know at the time was that I wouldn't be in the house next summer. One day Jake brought a puppy home and the girls were real excited about it. I never allowed a dog in the house. We had dogs before. Jake would bring them home and I was the one to take care of them. I was furious at Jake for bringing a puppy home. I was tired to begin with and things still weren't right in the house. Things kept disappearing. Being the softie I am, within hours I was cuddling the soft ball of fur and said yes about it staying in our house. It was strange, I put the puppy down in the kitchen and she made a bee line for the door. She began whining so we took her back outside. My niece's grandmother had a dog house for sale, so I went over and bought it. After Jake went to work that evening, everything started messing up again. I started blowing light bulbs once again. The garbage disposal that Jake fixed wouldn't work. I was upstairs brushing my teeth when the sink stopped up again. When I went to pull the chain to turn the light off, it kept coming back on. The thing that really got me was when I picked up the phone to call my mom, there was nothing. Not even a dial tone, just dead silence. What was going on around here?

It was around ten o'clock when I laid down. Well that didn't last long at all, again I was awakened. The talk show had just started. My eyes flew straight to the wall, just like a magnet. My heart started skipping beats. As always, I sat up waiting for daylight. Jake came home when the girls were eating breakfast. When the girls left for school, I went upstairs to talk to Jake. Scream is more like it. Needless to say, we got into a heated argument over the house. I told him I should have never listened to him about buying the house. It was my money and I should have gotten the house I wanted. He was still upstairs in the bedroom when I slammed out the door. Once outside, I started walking around the yard. Our puppy was jumping around. She was tied up by her dog house. I started walking toward her when all of the sudden I was pushed so hard, I almost fell to my knees. While turning around, I screamed, "you son of a bitch!" I was shocked to see no one there. No human could have pushed me that hard and been gone that quick. I looked at our playful puppy who now was as still as could be. She just stood there staring at me as if she was too scared to move. I ran in the house taking the stairs two at a time. Before my feet even hit the living room floor, I could hear Jake snoring. I knew Jake couldn't have pushed me and been gone that fast. Besides, if it was Jake, he would have stood there arguing, he sure wouldn't have left. I went back downstairs and looked at our puppy. I stood there wondering, what in the hell she saw push me that frightened her so much. Looking back, I should have left that house right then. I didn't though; I stayed and kept everything to myself.

Brett was coming over to play with the girls' everyday. I didn't mind, he was like the son I never had and he and the girls got along great. One day, I spent all day rearranging things. I worked like a mad woman. Late that night, I was still working around the house. It seemed like everything I had done, It hadn't satisfied me. I ran up and down the stairs until I was so exhausted I knew I had to quit. I still hadn't had much sleep lately. I laid on the couch and in seconds, I was out. Then it happened, I felt myself slipping away. I tried to stop it but it was too late. I was no sooner out of my body when I felt the pain. If I thought the first beating was bad, this was worse. I was hit and kicked over and over. I kept praying for God to help me. Finally it was over and I was back in my body. I knew for sure what had just happened. I also knew whoever was doing this to me was watching me and waiting for me to leave my body. It was smart enough to know that the only time I left my body was when I was exhausted. Is that why I was being awakened every night? To wear me down?

One morning I tried talking to Jake about what was going on. I told him our house was haunted but I didn't go into detail about what was happening to me. I just told him something bad was in the house. He said, "Every house you have lived in has been haunted." Most of the houses I had lived in were haunted but this was different, this was evil. Jake just laughed. If it was happening to him, he wouldn't be laughing. There was no use in discussing it any further. Jake wouldn't believe me anyway. About this time, the phone was going dead all of the time. I went to my moms and called the phone company. They sent a repair man out. He checked the phones and lines inside. He couldn't find anything wrong. There was nothing I could do about the phone. Sometimes it worked, sometimes it didn't.

Things weren't getting any better. I still wasn't sleeping at night. I would doze off and something would wake me up. The same talk show would be starting and my heart would skip those crazy beats. One day the girls brought the puppy inside the house. She sat right by the front door. The girls tried to get her in the kitchen. She finally gave in and came half way then turned around and ran out. When the puppy got bigger, they brought her in the house; the girls pulled her to the utility room. She cried like a baby and took off running. The girls were laughing. They pulled her by her Hind legs and began dragging her. At first, I was laughing until I saw how terrified she was. I began to scream at the girls to let her go. As soon as they released her legs, she ran out the front door. She sat there whining until we put her back outside. I knew in my heart that our dog could see things that we couldn't and I felt really sorry for her. The dog and I were the only ones who knew what was going on in the house.

 I decided there wasn't much I could do. I had already put a lot of money in the house, so whether I was comfortable with living there or not, I would have to learn to live with it. I tried to ignore the little things like my keys disappearing. One minute they would be on the kitchen table and the next thing I knew, they would be upstairs. Right before I moved in, I purchased a tape from the music store, it was a Michael McDonald tape. I played it almost everyday. One morning I went to play the tape and it wasn't there. I always put the tape up so I was shocked to find it was missing. I looked for hours, but still no sign of the tape. When the girls got home from school, I asked them if they had seen it, they said no. when Brett came over I asked him if he had picked it up or if he had seen it, again the answer was no. I looked for two days. I finally gave up and went back to the music store to buy another one. When I got back home I put the tape away and staring me in the face was the exact same tape. I couldn't believe it, that tape had not been there before. Things were missing all of the time. Some never appeared again.

 I called my sister one day and told her I had some exercise equipment that I didn't want and asked if she could come over to get it. Her and her son Tyler came to get it. When they got there, I was really disappointed because they didn't want to spend time with me. I was always real close to Tyler and he use to spend the night with us before. Now he seemed like he couldn't get out of the house fast enough. Since they had come all the way from Creve Core Missouri, I thought they would stay for awhile but they didn't. Oh well, my birthday was coming up so I knew they would be back, Maybe Tyler would change his mind and stay the weekend with us.

 Every night was still the same. I would go to sleep and then something would wake me up. The talk show would be starting and then I would sit there staring at the wall. My heart skipping its wild beats seemed to be getting worse. Jake and I were fighting more and more. One morning, after the girls left for school, Jake said, "Cindy, come here." I asked, "What do you want?" he repeated himself and I told him I was really tired. The next thing I knew, Jake had an oversized pillow over my face holding me down. I kicked him and tried to scream through the pillow. I couldn't breathe, I knew I had to get away from him but I didnt know if could. Jake was a big man; over 6 feet tall. I was so scared. finally I managed to get away. I grabbed my purse and keys and jumped into my van and took off. I found myself sitting in my mom's driveway crying. I sat there for awhile. I didn't want my mom to know what was going on. I calmed myself down and went in moms with all smiles. Haley had been staying at mom's house so she was there. I was glad she was there; I needed someone to talk to. I told Haley what had happened but I asked her not to tell mom. I spent the day at mom's house. When it was time for the girls to be home from school, I waited at the bus stop for them. I sat there thinking about what happened to me earlier that morning. I remembered the strange look on Jake's face and the far away look in his eyes. I dreaded going back to the house, but I knew I had to. When the girls got off the bus, we headed up the hill. Jake was awake when we came in. I never mentioned what had happened and neither did he.

Everything was still the same, lights dimming and me getting awakened by something I couldnt see. On my birthday, October 10, Sydney, Brett, Lindsey, and I were outside. The kids were drawing with chalk on the patio area. Lindsey came running over to me crying. I asked her what was wrong. She repeated something Brett had said to her. It sent chills down my spine. He said, "I'm going to nail your mom to the wall at midnight." I asked Brett why he had said that and he had an odd look on his face and shrugged his shoulders and said he didn't know. By the look on his face, I could tell he really didn't know why. I told him that wasn't a nice thing to say and he had scared Lindsey. I also told him never to talk like that anymore.

It was right after that, that things really got worse in the house. I gave the girls their baths and tucked them in bed. I had already taken my bath. I got on the couch and said my prayers and welcomed two hours of sleep that I desperately needed. I was sleeping when someone pulled my eyelash, hard enough to hurt. I said owe! I looked around but no one was there. I looked at the clock and I hadn't even been sleeping an hour. I put my arm over my eyes and began to fall asleep. I was so tired. All of the sudden, I was hit in the arm real hard. It felt like someone hit me with their fist. I said, "What the hell!" I looked around but no one was there. My eyes went to the wall. By now, I was sitting up, no longer tired. My heart was skipping beats. When daylight came, I pretended that everything was normal in front of

Jake and the girls. When the girls left for school, I tried to talk to Jake. He blew me off like always, everything was a big joke to him. I wondered if anybody would believe me if I told them.

I called my mom one evening and she said that my sister and my nephew Tyler were over there and they had my birthday present with them. I told mom to tell them to come over. Mom said that Taylor was going to leave the gift at her house and I could come and get it. I told mom to put her on the phone. I begged my sister to come over. I finally talked her into coming over. When they arrived, I asked Tyler if he wanted to spend the weekend with us, he said he didn't want to. Since he would spend weeks at a time with us before, I didn't understand his strange behavior. The girls really missed him but all their begging didn't help. They stayed long enough for me to open my gift and they were gone. I felt like crying.

I moved here to be closer to my mom but I was always too tired to even visit her. My whole purpose of moving back to Caseyville was to be near her and help her. Everything was so crazy. The only sleep I got was when Jake was off work for two nights. But even then as tired as I was, I was afraid of getting hit. Or worse, leaving my body and getting beat again. The girls would sleep on the couch the nights when I would sleep with Jake. At first, Jake was mad about them being on the couch and made them sleep in their room. They tried but they were just too scared. They complained to me about it. Most of the time, Jake and I would get into an argument and he would end up going to his mothers and sleeping there.

Things went from bad to worse with Jake and I. I sometimes wondered if this evil thing wasn't somehow controlling him. One night after I got the kids tucked in for bed, I was laying on the couch and had just said my prayers. I was looking at the wall. I said nothing out loud, I was just thinking to myself. My thoughts were saying, "I know you're in there so why don't you show yourself? It's not fair you can see me and I can't see you." Right after that, I fell asleep. Sleep didn't last long. I was punched so hard. I opened my eyes and looked at the wall. Staring back at me was a small boy. He looked a lot like my nephew Tyler. He was dressed really different though, like maybe in the early thirties. He had a black beanie cap on, a white shirt with a beige vest, beige khaki pants to the knees, and black stockings from the knees down. His shoes were black with a strap across them. We were just staring at one another. I wasn't frightened by him at all. Maybe it was because he looked so much like Tyler. He motioned for me to follow him. It was as if I could read his mind. He didn't speak to me but I knew he wanted me to play with him. I felt like everything was drained out of me as I watched him go around the corner and disappear. My eyes felt like lead and I did sleep that night. I slept around five hours. That was the longest I had slept since I got in the house. The next morning, I stood where the little boy was. The bunk beds were there and I wondered where he went. He either went straight through the wall to where the girls were or he went back into the wall he came out of. I wondered how a small boy his size could be beating the hell out of me. I had my doubts. His small body couldn't have the strength that whatever was attacking me had. If it isn't the boy, then who was it? And why did it want to hurt me?

Things went on the same. I was still getting awakened and my heart kept skipping beats. I was also still being punched but the little boy never appeared again. One day a friend of mine named Cathy came by. I knew she didn't like the house by the look on her face. She said something about it being dark inside the house. After I gave her a tour of the house, we sat down in the kitchen. She asked me what was wrong. "You look so tired and worn out" she said. Even though we knew each other since the fourth grade, I knew she wouldn't understand what was going on. After all, I couldn't understand it myself. I wasn't about to tell anybody how crazy my life had become. I told her that I had been fighting with Jake. After Cathy left, I sat there thinking about everything that was going on in the house. I was always told I had a big heart and I always tried to help others when I could. I always put other's needs before my own. So why did this thing hate me so much? Why did it keep hurting me? That night, Jake flew into another rage. I think it started when Kendra came over and asked me to stop by her work if I wasn't doing anything. I would have loved to go, just to get away from the house. Jake never allowed me to go anywhere.

When Jake was getting ready for work, he was screaming at the top of his lungs. I walked outside and he started yelling at me. He was acting crazy again. I looked over at Kendra and her windows were open. I knew Bruce and Brett could hear what was going on and I was so embarrassed. Jake was still yelling at me as he was pulling down the hill. I knew he was mad when Kendra came over but that was hours ago. I really can't remember what set him off before he left for work. It seemed like he was always screaming and yelling at me lately. I stood outside the house. I would have given anything just to be able to get in my van and drive away but I had my girls to think about. I couldn't just drag them off through the night. I dreaded walking back into the house. God only knew what was waiting for me in there. Bruce came running out of Kendras and asked if I was ok. I told him that Jake went to work so I would be alright, he didn't have to worry about him the rest of the night. What I didn't tell Bruce was that something much more evil and powerful was waiting for me inside.

I was still getting awakened every night but the evil thing started getting rougher, hitting me harder to wake me up. My heart continued to skip beats but now something else was happening. My ears would close up when this thing was around me. When I would feel its presence around me, I could hardly hear. One Saturday morning Jake yelled, "Cindy, do you think the TV is loud enough?" I looked at the girls and asked them if it was loud. They replied, "Yes mommy, it's real loud but its ok." They felt bad Jake was yelling at me again. I walked over to the TV and turned it down. I asked them if they could hear it and they said yes. They could hear it but I couldn't. This evil thing was coming out in the daytime now. My heart was skipping those wild beats through the day but only when it was present. I thanked God that it wasn't hitting me or pushing me in front of the children.

    A group of women I knew had a yard sale twice a year. They were in a really good location. It was right on the Main Street in Caseyville. They said I was welcomed to join them. I called mom and Ann and asked them if they had anything to put in the sale, they both said yes. Jake said, "You're not going anywhere, you have no business sitting down there on Main Street." I always did what Jake asked but this time I had enough. I started going through things to tag, that really made Jake mad. I only had a few days until the sale and this time I was going to do something I wanted to do. Jake couldn't handle that and the next day all hell broke loose. Jake had been screaming like he was crazy. I went upstairs to get something when I noticed that Jake was drinking. I asked him,"What the hell are you doing?" After getting called a few choice names, I knew I was in big trouble this time. I prayed the phone wasn't dead again and for once it was working. I called his mom and my mom and told them I needed help. They both came over. Jake's mom talked him into going home with her and spending the night. My mom was still worried he would come back. I said I'd be ok and she could go home. She said no that she would stick around just in case. It was dark out when we heard someone screaming and cussing like a mad man. He was back. I had the doors locked. Jake was trying to break the door down! I told him to leave and that I was calling the police. He kept it up, so I called the police. They said they were sending someone to my house. They still haven't arrived when Jake came around the corner with an ax. I called the police station back, telling them to hurry that he had an ax. About that time, the police came up the hill. Jake still had the ax in his hand. There were more than one police car. One officer jumped out of his car and asked Jake what he was doing with an ax. Jake replied, "I was chopping wood" The policeman said, "Not this late at night your not"" he told Jake to put down the ax. He took a light and shined it in Jake's eyes, then he asked him for his car keys. They ended up driving him back to his mom's house.

A few days later we set a time up for a police officer to be at my house while Jake got his belongings out. Jake's car had been broken down. I knew he needed transportation to and from work. Since I owned a nice car and a van, I told him I would sign my car over to him. He had been drinking a lot more lately, so the agreement was that he wouldn't bother me anymore. Everybody told me not to sign my car over to him but I did anyway. That was another mistake. Jake would walk back and forth down the road until the girl's would see him. He finally got to the girls; they loved him and missed him. I finally agreed to talk to him. He promised to quit drinking if I gave him a second chance. I told him I needed time to think it through. As for the drinking, Jake drank a lot when I first met him. One night I told him I wasn't raising Sydney around someone who drank, that wasn't what I wanted for her. Jake quit drinking after I told him that. So maybe he would quit now although I wasn't so sure.

When I went down to the yard sale, Jake kept driving around. I was so afraid Jake would cause a scene so I ended up leaving. Things were still the same in the house. One night after getting two hours of sleep, I was punched harder than the last time. Some nights I was punched in the stomach or hit on the arm. So being punched when I was awake wasn't so bad. This particular night I was awakened, I looked at the wall and was shocked to find a man standing there. He was on the opposite side of where the little boy had appeared. He was tall with dark hair. He was a very handsome man. He looked to be in his late twenties or early thirties. He was dressed in a white shirt with puffy sleeves and he had dark pants that were tucked into knee boots. I felt as if he had fought in some kind of a war. There was something on the side of him; it was either a sword or a rifle. I didn't see it until after we made eye contact. When we made eye contact, I was so afraid. His eyes held evil and hatred. frightened, I turned my head, wishing he would leave. When I looked again, he was gone. I sat there the rest of the night wondering if he was the one that was beating me. Then I remembered the flag pole outside by the front entrance. Jake and I had fought over the flag. It had been up there for years and it had holes in it. It was real worn out. I asked Jake to take it down. He didn't want to but I told him I would get a new one. With all of the fighting going on between us, we never got around to replacing it. I don t think it was even down a week. I began to wonder if that's what made the soldier mad. I also wondered how many people were in that wall. A day or two later, Jake was walking back and fourth again unshaven and crying. The girls really felt bad for him. I was beginning to soften myself.

One night after being awakened, I tried to avoid the wall. Instead of looking at it, I began watching the talk show. On a commercial break, I went to the bathroom. As I was washing my hands, I looked in the mirror. I gasped at what I saw. The woman in the mirror wasn't me. She was old with thin gray hair; her eyes and face were sunk in. Her face was all wrinkled up. I went to pull the chain to turn the light off but it came back on. When I pulled it again, I felt someone pulling with me. I left the chain swinging back in fourth with the light still on. I ran out of the bathroom. I sat on the couch and stared at the wall. I wondered if I was losing my mind. I knew one thing, if I ever had to use the bathroom again; I would hold it until it was daylight.

Jake stopped by when I was getting the kids ready for school. I decided to let him stay. We talked awhile and got along real good. Jake never moved all of his belongings back in but he was staying with us again. One morning after being up all night, I had to go to the bathroom. It was daylight so I felt safe. I was in the bathroom when I heard what sounded like a gunshot. I ran out of the bathroom and stood in the living room. I looked up at the ceiling to find a part of it was hanging down. I just stood there laughing. I knew I couldn't take much more. It was either breakdown and cry or laugh, I chose to laugh. It wasn't a normal laugh but a hysterical one instead. I needed to pull myself together; I had to get the girls up for school. I calmed myself down and did what I had to do. While the girls were having their breakfast, I showed Jake the ceiling and he said he would fix it.

I can only remember one time that anything really funny happened while I was living in that house. I hadn't gotten the girls up for school yet, I was downstairs cooking them breakfast when I heard a knock at the door. I wondered who could be coming over so early. I opened the door and there stood Brett. I said, "Honey, the girls aren't even up yet. It's too early." Brett said, "Cindy, I know, I just wanted to eat breakfast with you." That's when I noticed he had two pieces of buttered toast on a plate. I told him to come on in. I asked him if his mother knew he had come over and he said yes. It wasn't like Kendra to send him over that early. A few minutes later the phone rang, it was Kendra. It seemed Brett had gotten up before she did. She told me to send Brett home, that he was in big trouble. I, myself thought it was funny him bringing toast over so we could have breakfast together.

The house itself was driving me crazy. I still hadn't put everything together what was happening to me. I noticed a big change in the girls. Sydney always seemed frightened. She was always close to me whenever possible. As for Lindsey, she was always a whiner but other than that, she was a good kid. Lately she was acting different towards me. One night she was really acting up. My nerves were on edge as it was. She kept pushing me until I finally spanked her. She began hitting and kicking me. I couldn't believe Lindsey had struck me. I looked over at Sydney and she began crying. She told Lindsey to stop. It seemed like forever before Lindsey calmed down. As I looked at my daughters, I knew this house was destroying us little by little.

Haley stopped by one evening and decided to stay the night. I was so happy to know that another adult would be with me that night. When it was time to go to bed, Haley wanted to sleep downstairs in the T.V. room. I explained to her that the girls slept in my room and I slept on the couch. I told her she could take Lindsey and Sydney's room but for some reason she declined the offer for their bedroom. In a way, I was glad because I wouldn't want anything to happen to Haley. On the other hand, I wanted her upstairs so maybe she could see what was happening to me. The next morning Haley said, "Cindy, I didn't sleep all night." I asked her why? She said that it felt like someone was in the room with her. She said she couldn't see anyone but she could feel it. I said, "Haley, I wish you would of came upstairs, I was up all night too. This house is strange and I never get any sleep." That's all that was said, it was time to get the girls up. While I was getting their breakfast ready, I thought about what Haley had said. I was glad she picked up on whatever she did. Just because it never bothered Jake, didn't mean it didn't exist.

I was shocked one day when the phone rang. It was a friend of mine, Allie who I hadn't spoken to since I moved back to Caseyville. We met in second grade and had remained friends through the years. She called to tell me that she was working in a hotel and they needed help really bad. I said, "Allie, I would love to but you know how my back is. I could try part time." she said she would help me with my rooms so my back wouldn't go out. When I hung up the phone, I wondered how I was going to manage working without any sleep. It was hard enough just trying to function around the house. I was so tired all of the time that I couldn't even make myself visit my mom. Every time I even thought about going, I would feel so weak. I would end up staying home. It was like this thing was trying to keep me from my mom. It was smart. Looking back, maybe it knew I would tell my mom what was going on. I was always close to her and I had always told her everything up until now. For what ever reason, this thing did not want me at my moms house. So I remained a prisoner in my own home. Well I was tired of being a prisoner. Besides, we could use the extra money. When Jake woke up, I told him about the job. Of course he was against it. My place, according to him was right here in the house taking care of him and the children. We fought for hours over it. When I told him I was going to put my application in and that I would be right back, he really came unglued. I finally said, "Forget it, I won't go!" Jake was satisfied but I wasn't.

Jake fell asleep before the girls got home from school so I picked up the girls and I got an application. I hid the application until he went to work. When he was gone, I filled it out. I knew I would have to take it in at night, it was already so late so I explained to the girls what I was doing and they were all for it. So we piled in the van and we were on our way. When I turned the application into the night clerk, I made some excuse about why I brought it in so late at night. She said that it was fine and that she would make sure it got in the right hands in the morning. I told the girls to keep their fingers crossed that I get the job. A few days later, I got a call that I was hired. I would start the following week.

I decided with my heart skipping beats, that I would get a physical to ease my mind. I called and got an appointment the very next day. When the nurse was hooking me up to an EKG machine, I looked at her and wanted to ask her if she believed in ghosts. I wanted to tell her I thought a ghost had something to do with my heart skipping beats. The funny thing was, since I was away from the house, my heart wasn't skipping beats. I opened my mouth to speak but nothing came out. As she was leaving the room, I was glad I didn't say anything. After all, she didn't really even know me. She would probably think I was crazy. When the doctor came in, he said he wanted to run some more tests. One was because I took water pills, so he wanted to check my bladder and kidneys. Everything turned out fine. He said my EKG was ok also. At least there was nothing wrong that had showed up. He said he could run some more tests on my heart but they would be very expensive and I didn't have any insurance. For the tests he ran today, I was paying cash and they would have set me back enough. We agreed if I ever got insurance then he would run further tests. When I walked out of the office, I knew the ghost was causing these problems. I couldn't wait to get out of the prison and start working. When I told Jake I was hired and was starting work, he was mad. I didn't care, I would start early in the morning and be home in time for the girls. So while the girls were getting ready for school, I was getting ready for work. I would take the girls to the bus stop and go straight to work. I was hired part time but I was putting more hours in. My back was hurting but I loved the extra money and Allie always said she would help me.

I still wasn't sleeping and one day after I got off work, I was extremely exhausted. I opened the door to the house and smelled wood burning. I took the steps two at a time. One of my worst fears yet was the fireplace. There it was, blazing away. I had told Jake never to light the fireplace. I asked him why he had lit it. He just looked at me. I was too tired to argue. Jake laid on the bed reading the newspaper. My back hurt badly so I rubbed some medicine on it and laid on the bed next to Jake. I closed my eyes and started drifting off, I felt myself slipping out of my body. I remember thinking no but it was too late. The next thing I knew was that I was running, someone was chasing me. I made it to the stairs. I was half way down when I looked into my kitchen. What had happened to my kitchen? It was now a laboratory. Who were these two men? They had white lab coats on. One man had a test tub shaking it up and down. They were talking about what was in the test tube. I watched their lips move but I couldn't hear what was being said. I saw myself also but I was dressed different. I looked like someone that was working in a coal mine. I had some kind of a band around my head with a light on it. The light was turned on. I wondered what the hell was going on. I ran up the steps. Oh God, I was getting the worst beating I had ever gotten. It went on and on. Then when I thought I couldn't take anymore, it began hitting me harder and harder. Then when I tried to go back in my body, I was pulled back out. It felt like when a dentist is pulling the root a tooth that's stuck; only this was a hundred times worse. I could actually feel myself passing through my body. The bones in my face hurt, I could hear them making a cracking noise. I couldn't believe the pressure and the strength this thing had. I didn't stand a chance. I asked God to help me. The more I prayed, the harder it pulled. While I was being pulled, I heard a mans voice say, "Its evil, its evil." He kept repeating this. I kept thinking through all this pain, oh God please help me! I don't want to die! I kept praying, "in the name of Jesus, please help me!" I repeated this prayer over and over. After what seemed like an eternity, it finally let go. I was now back in my body. I sat up and looked around. Jake was still reading the newspaper. I asked Jake if he had seen anything. "When I was sleeping, did you see me moving around?" he looked at me as if I were crazy. I told him never mind. I walked into the living room and looked at the fireplace. I was still standing there when Jake walked into the room. I looked at him and said, "Don't you ever light that fireplace again!" He said, "What is wrong with you?" I replied, "Jake, I told you before not to light it but you did anyway. If you ever do it again, you and I are through for good." Somehow by Jake lighting the fireplace, it gave this evil being more strength. I also knew that without a doubt that this thing was trying to kill me. I was so scared that I was afraid to even try to sleep my two hours at night. I knew I had to get some sleep though but every time I would get tired, I would think about the last beating. The thing had gone for my lower back and my stomach. It hurt my back the worst. It felt like it was kicking me in the kidneys. I also kept thinking, what if this time it wouldn't let me go back in my body? I didn't want to die but I didn't know how to fight this thing. Since I started working, I guess I made this evil thing mad because I wasn't in the house 24 hours a day. My punishment was being stuck with what felt like a needle or I would get burned with what felt like a lit cigarette. Every time I would get stuck or burned, it would hurt and always made me jump. The weird thing about it was, it never left a mark.

This evil thing was not only powerful but it was smart as well. One day my cousin Will came by with his girlfriend Kelly. Jake was up and sitting at the kitchen table. We were all sitting there talking when the phone rang. When I answered the phone, a man was on the line. He said, "Can you talk Cindy?" I asked, "who is this?" Then the phone went dead. Since I had an unlisted number and didn't recognize the voice, I thought it was strange. For once, Jake didn't question who was on the phone. He just kept talking to Will. They stayed for awhile then they left.

One day the reception was really messed up on the TV, it was a weekend and the girls were home. Jake decided to climb on the roof and fix the antenna. Sydney and Lindsey were playing with Brett. Lindsey came running over to me with a frightened look on her face. She said, "Mom, Brett said he was going to split dads head open with a tool he has." I looked up towards the roof and noticed Jake was staring at us and had heard what was said. I walked over to Brett; he was sitting on the ground. He had a large tool in his hand. I said, "Brett, you didn't say you were going to split Jake's head open did you?" I waited for Brett's answer. I almost fell over when he looked me straight in the eyes and said "Yeah I said it and I'm going to do it." He had the tool in his hand moving it back and forth. I took the tool from Brett's hand. I didn't even notice that Jake had come down off the roof. I was so shocked by Brett's behavior that all I could hear or see was Brett. Jake was right behind me yelling at Brett to stay in his own yard. I liked Brett and I felt bad that Jake was yelling at him. I also knew though that it wasn't right for what Brett had said.

On Monday when the girls got off the school bus, their faces had a weird expression on them and I knew that something was wrong. Brett had spit in their hair. They had just washed their hair the night before. The idea that Brett had done something like that to the girls really made me mad. I went over to talk to Kendra about Brett's behavior. Brett answered the door. Kendra wasn't home, Janet was babysitting. Brett said he was sorry and he would never do it again. When Kendra got home, she came over and talked to me about Brett. She said the night before, she caught him playing with matches and he told her when she went to sleep, he was going to burn their trailer down, she said she didn't know what to do so she was going to get him counseling. She said she called and said it was an emergency and they got him right in

Our dog was another problem I was having. Kendra called one night telling me the dog was crying and barking a lot at night. Kendra said no one was outside because she checked to see. I told Kendra the dog wouldn't come in the house so I didn't know what to do. I started checking on her often since I was awake all night anyway. I always gave our dog a bucket of water every night but by morning, she would wrap her chain around it and it would be empty. Since she was much bigger now, I started filling a five gallon bucket full. It was much heavier but still by morning, it would be laying on the ground empty. I went out one morning prepared to fill her bucket. I stopped in my tracks when I saw the bucket was on the other side of the yard without a drop of water out of it. I looked at the full bucket of water and then at the dog. I said, "How did you do that?" There was no way she could have moved that bucket without knocking it over. Every night I would put fresh water in the bucket and every morning it would be moved across the yard, full.

One night she was making a lot of noise, so I went down stairs and turned the porch light on. I walked outside. It was as if she were waiting for me. I looked at her and she stood there looking back at me. Her brown eyes had a green glow. I was horrified, I ran back in the house. The next morning when I went out I found the bucket on the other side of the yard. It was as full as it was when I had first filled it. But I saw something else, which looked liked giant footprints. They were all around where the dog was. Something was very wrong here.

At night, my light switches started shooting electricity out at me. If I was afraid of the house catching on fire before, I was really terrified now. I called my uncle Tim. since he lived next door to my mom, I thought he would come over and try to fix it or have his friend who did electrical work. When I needed the 210 wiring put in for the dryer, I had paid him to do it. Tim had come over with his friend back then but he started shaking and saying he couldn't breathe. He ran out the door. So I thought he was just sick that day. When I spoke to him on the phone I was really hurt when he said, "You will be alright tonight. When Jake gets off work tomorrow morning just have him tighten the screws." Half the time Jake wasn't even there anymore, we were fighting so badly. Jake came over the next morning and tightened the screws. I was still upset. My light bulbs were still blowing and the ones that weren't, were dimming.

One day when Jake was over, I was in the bedroom when suddenly I had the worst pain in my stomach. I didn't want Jake to know how bad it was hurting. The pain got so bad I doubled up and fell on the bed. Jake asked, "What's wrong?" I could hardly speak it hurt so badly. Just as quick as it had started, it had stopped. About a week later, I was in the bedroom again and Jake had just walked in the room. I was fine one minute and the next I was doubled over in pain again. Jake got really upset this time and said he wanted to get me to a doctor to be checked. I said that I would. I never made an appointment though. Why waste more money and time? A doctor couldn't help what was going on with me. I knew it was the evil thing. It didn't want me and Jake together unless we were fighting.

Tim's daughter, my cousin Elizabeth came by one day. The girls had let her in. I was upstairs with Jake when they came running up the stairs excited because she had come over. All of the sudden, I felt sick to my stomach, and then the pain started. My head hurt so badly. I could hardly stand the pain. I crawled on my hands and knees to get to the bathroom. With every movement, the pain shot through my head. The girls took one look at me and asked, "Mom, what's wrong?" Jake said, "your mom is sick, go tell Elizabeth she will have to come back another time." I stayed in the bathroom most of the afternoon.

One night I was drying clothes. I was using the dryer a lot more now because it was November. It was working fine but all of the sudden, it stopped. I walked over and hit the circuit breaker, I still had nothing. I had to dry my uniform for work the next morning so I hung it up on hangers. Since it wasn't the circuit, I was going to have to buy a new dryer. Maybe I didn't have to buy a new one, this dryer wasn't that old. Maybe it wouldn't cost that much to get fixed, at the least I was hoping anyway. When Jake walked in the next morning, I told him that the dryer had gone out. He walked over to where the circuit was and hit it. The dryer came on. I stood there dumbfounded. I had done the same thing last night but it didn't work for me.

The next night was worse. The girls and I had stayed downstairs longer than usual. I had a bad feeling about the house all evening. All hell was about to break loose and I could feel it. Electricity started coming out of the light switches downstairs. I took a screw driver and tightened the screws myself, but it didn't help. I dreaded going upstairs that night. The girls had school the next morning and I had to work. I needed my two hours of sleep. When we first moved in, I had hung a picture of Jesus as you were walking up the stairs. As I approached the steps, the picture was staring me right in the face. I stopped and touched the picture. I prayed aloud, "In Jesus name, please bless this house. Bless Sydney, Lindsey and myself and please watch over us, Amen." The girls took their baths. I told them they could stay up a little while longer. I wanted to take a bath also. I didn't take mine that day like I usually did. I left the bathroom door opened and tried to hurry. When I was through with my bath, I told the girls it was time for bed. I tucked the girls in and kissed them and told them I loved them. As I laid down on the couch for my two hours of sleep, I didn't know that this would be the last night I would ever sleep in the house again. I said my prayers and felt my eyelids grow heavier and heavier. Next thing I knew, I was awakened. I looked at the TV. and the talk show was already over. I couldn't believe this evil thing had let me sleep. I had been living in this house for two months and every night I was awakened at the exact same time. I looked over at the wall. When I turned to look at the TV, I saw something moving out of the corner of my eye. I looked back at the wall; pinkish smoke was coming out of it. My first thought was, I was being warned of a fire. At first, only a small amount was coming out. I got up to get a closer look and that's when it started pouring out of the wall. It started taking form. Now it was a huge cloud, I couldn't believe what I was seeing. In the middle of this cloud was energy. The power and the strength this thing held was unbelievable. I was so frightened I couldn't move. I knew at that moment what had been beating me. The living room lights started flickering and the sound of the living room TV was coming in and out. This thing was pulling electricity from everywhere. I said, "God please help me. In Jesus name don't let these lights go out." I watched as this evil thing passed through the wall. It was going into the room my daughters were in. My first thought was that I had to get out of there. I looked toward the stairs. I thought to myself, "If I go downstairs then I will have to go passed the wall. No, I can't go by the wall because it might come back and attack me when I walked past." I looked around the room, the only way out was to jump through the window. I was getting ready to jump when I stopped dead in my tracks. What kind of a mother am I? I asked myself. My girls are in there with that thing. I asked God to please help me. I was in the middle of the room praying aloud when Lindsey came running out of the bedroom. Her face was twisted in anger and in a deep voice that was not her own she yelled, "I saw what you did and I hate you!" I said, "Mommy didn't do anything Lindsey." She repeated it again. I felt the tears roll down my cheeks as I said, "Please stop Lindsey! I didn't do anything!" right then I was terrified of my own daughter. I walked towards her, her eyes didn't look right; they had a far away look in them. No matter how afraid I was of the thing inside Lindsey, she was still my daughter. I put my arm around her and turned her around and said, "Come on Lindsey, go back to bed." When we walked in the bedroom, I noticed their light was off. That light was on when they went to sleep. I reached over and turned it back on. I tucked Lindsey back into bed. I stood there looking at Lindsey. That wasn't my daughter. Yes, it was her body but that twisted face and deep voice belonged to someone else. I went back into the living room. I looked at the clock, it was going on five a.m. Two people came into my mind, my uncle Todd and my Grandmother. Both were very religious. Todd was very active in church and grandma taught me about God at a very early age. When I was young, we would walk to church every Sunday. The church wasn't down the street either, it was miles away. It didn't matter how cold or how hot it was, grandma never let anything stop her from going to church. She taught me a lot about God but she also told me a lot about the devil. I was told if I wasn't good, the devil would get me. So as I sat there, I wondered what I did wrong. Grandma always went to bed early, therefore she got up early. I felt the need to talk to her. As I pushed the buttons on the phone, I prayed I wouldn't wake her up. I said out loud, "please grandma, be awake." she picked up the phone right away. I could tell by her voice, she had been awake for awhile. Just hearing her voice made me feel better. I said, "Grandma, I'm scared." She asked, "Cindy, what's wrong?" I told her what had just taken place. She said, "Cindy, you need to get out of that house now. There is something evil in there." I told her that I knew that and things have been happening since the very first day I had moved in. I just didn't tell anyone. I told her I couldn't explain everything now because I had to get ready for work then get the girls up for school. I told grandma that I wanted to talk to Uncle Todd but I didn't want to call and wake him up this early. I asked her to call mom later for me and explain to her what had happened to me. I also told her to tell her I was coming over right after work. I thanked her for listening to me. I told her I loved her and we hung up the phone. I went to check my curling brush to see if it was hot enough to curl my hair. I had plugged it in before I called my grandma. There it sat, unplugged. I plugged it back in then sat for a minute. By now, Haley was up because she had to get ready for work. I called her and started telling her what had happened. She screamed, "Cindy, shut up! I'm by myself and you're scaring me." I told her I was going to moms after I get off work. We hung up. Now it was time to wake the girls. I wanted to see how Lindsey acted when she got up. She seemed fine. I waited until breakfast and then I asked her if she remembered getting up earlier. She replied, "No." of course Lindsey wouldn't remember because it wasn't really Lindsey. I was glad she didn't know what had taken place.

When Jake came in I said, "Jake I'm going to go to my moms after work." he asked, "for what?" I told him because there was something evil in the house and it was trying to kill me. Jake said, "Oh come on Cindy!" I told him I didn't care whether he believed me or not. I also told him he had no idea what was going on and that I was leaving the house and I wasn't coming back. The girls had come back in the kitchen; they had gone to get their backpacks. I said, "Come on or you will miss the bus." we hurried out of the house. I drove down the hill and waited for the girls to get on the bus. Before they got out of the car, I told them to take the bus to grandma's house after school. Sydney asked, "why mom? Where will you be?" I told her I would be at grandmas because I had to talk to her about something. I told them to make sure they didn't go home because daddy would be sleeping. When the bus arrived, I watched the girls get on the bus and I knew they were safe because they were away from the house.

    I pulled onto the road and started driving to work. I thought about the big cloud of energy and the power it had. It was so smart. It was controlling everyone in the house one way or another. Why did it hate me so much? I knew it wanted me to die. I thanked God for thoughts of my children that morning because if I would have jumped out of the window, I know I would have without a doubt, bled to death from the glass or broke my neck from the fall. I'm surprised I didn't die from pure fright. Maybe the day it tried to keep me out of my body, it was mad because it didn't succeed. So it was going to find other ways to kill me. I remembered the mans voice that day repeating, "Its evil, It's evil." My grandma had said the same thing. I needed to talk to my uncle Todd. Surely the church would have someone who could pray it out.

    I pulled into the parking lot at work. I sat there a few minutes and wiped the fresh hot tears off my face. I looked terrible. I went downstairs to clock in. I always considered myself to be a fairly strong person. I had been through a lot in my lifetime. Today I felt different. I felt weak and confused. I asked God to give me the strength to get through work today. Allie was waiting for me downstairs. It only took one look when Allie asked me what was wrong. "You look like you seen a ghost" she added. I tried to speak but no words would come out. I tried again but I was studdering so bad I could hardly talk, I never studdered in my life. I told Allie what had happened as best as I could and I hoped she could understand me. The frightened look on her face told me she could. It was dark in the basement and it was scary. Allie said, "Come on Cindy, let's get out of here. I said I didn't want anyone to see me like this. Allie didn't tell me she thought I was crazy, she believed me right from the start just like my grandma did. Allie was by my side all day long and if someone would ask a question, she made sure she answered it. I was usually friendly with all our co-workers but today was different. Allie did all of the talking and saved me a lot of embarrassment. I tried to avoid everyone all day.

    Well, I had made it through work, now it was time to face my mom and tell her what had been going on. When I pulled in the driveway, Haley was there. I got out of the van and walked in. Mom was staring at me and

Haley had a big grin on her face. I knew that grandma had called mom so why was she looking at me so weird? As for Haley, I wanted to smack that grin right off her face. Mom said, "Sit down and tell me what's going on." I said, "Mom, if I go back home, I'm going to die." It took forever just to get that much out of me. The look on my mom's face was pure shock when she asked, "why can't you talk?" It was like a dam burst inside of me, I cried and cried and I couldn't stop. Finally when I calmed down enough, I told her some of what had been going on since I moved in the house. I couldn't tell her everything at once, I could hardly talk to begin with. I had moved in the house early September. It was now the second week of November. I had been living in hell for almost 10 weeks. Mom agreed to let me and the girls stay with her until I could contact someone to get the evil thing out. After everything that had went on I wondered if I could ever live there again.

The phone suddenly rang and mom answered it. It was my uncle Todd and he wanted to talk to me. He said that grandma explained everything to him. He said he had called every church he could think of and they all said the same thing. What I had described was the devil himself and it was too evil, they were not prayed up enough to go into the house. I began to cry again. I said, "Todd you mean that no one will help me? If I go back there I will die! It will kill me!" when I hung up from Todd I decided to call a priest from a local church. He acted as if this were some kind of a joke. He said he would meet with me in a few days and then we would talk about it. What was wrong with him? I might not have a few days. What if this thing could leave the hill and find me? The phone rang again. Mom answered it and talked for awhile. When she was finished she handed me the phone and told me it was Jake. I tried to speak the best I could. Jake said, "Cindy, what the hell is going on? Why can't you talk right?" He wanted to come over and talk to me in person. I said, "No Jake, I don't want to see you right now."

The girls came to moms after school just like they were told to. When they walked in, my eyes were swollen. When I tried to talk to them, I scared them. Mom sat the girls down and tried to explain what was going on. Sydney said she already knew about the evil thing. I said, "Oh no, did it ever hurt you?" she said, no, that she could just feel it around her all the time. She said she would get goose bumps and she would get real cold when it was around. She also said that one night she was lying in bed with her eyes closed and it felt like she floated up to the ceiling. Why hadn't I paid more attention to that frightened look on her face? Thank God it hadn't hit her. She said it felt like someone was always watching her. Lindsey didn't have much to say. I paced back and forth wondering what I had done to make it mad enough to speak through Lindsey. "I saw what you did and I hate you." What had I done? I still didn't know. Someone was knocking on the door, it was Jake. I ran in my mom's bedroom and shut the door. Mom came in and told me that Jake wanted to talk to me. I said, "No, I asked him not to come here!" What if this thing followed him? I was so scared. Mom said that Jake was upset when he had left. He was upset? Well, what about me? My nerves were shot and I would jump at every little noise. The phone rang again and it was Uncle Todd. He told me he had called back because he decided he was going to pray it out himself. I said, "No, Todd. I couldn't live with myself if something happened to you because of me. Todd, I felt it and I saw it. I know how powerful it is. I was beat so bad that I thought I was going to die. No Todd, whoever goes in there will have to be experienced in this type of thing." I could only pray that there was such a person. Before we hung up, Todd told me to get my mom's bible and turn it to Psalms 91" and read 1-16 aloud. He said it was important that I have everyone in the house sit with me when I read it. Before he hung up, he asked me what talk show was on when I was getting woken up. I told him the name of the talk show. The phone rang a few minutes later and it was Todd again. He said, "Cindy, you were getting woken up at exactly midnight, the bewitching hour. Get the bible and start praying now." I told my mom what Todd had just said. I told her that he looked up the show in the TV guide. We got mom's bible out and gathered around and started reading aloud Psalms 91'.

Later I went to the mini mart up the street. When I walked in, I was hoping I wouldn't run into anyone I knew. There was no way I could carry on a conversation with someone. When I got back to moms, my Uncle Randy was just pulling up. He took one look at me and asked, "Cindy, what's wrong?" I wished people would quit asking me that because it always brought tears to my eyes. I felt the tears rolling down my cheeks. I looked at Randy and said, "You wouldn't believe me if I told you." He said, "come on Cindy, tell me what's wrong." I started telling him a little bit of what was going on in the house when I stopped. Randy said, "I believe you ." I was close to Randy when I was younger but I didn't know if he believed in ghosts. That was something we had never discussed. Randy had brought his girlfriend Jennifer over to the house several times but I had always acted like everything was fine. So I just assumed he would think I was crazy. I thought everyone would think I lost my mind but so far everyone believed me. Randy and I walked down the sidewalk and walked into moms together. I was talking to the girls when I overheard mom saying, "I don't know, she hasn't been able to speak right since this morning." By the time Randy had left, it was getting late. Since mom only had one bedroom in her apartment, the girls were to sleep with her tonight. As for me, I was to sleep on the couch. The girls were off school the next day but I was scheduled to work. When everyone was fast asleep, I was awake. I thought about the evil thing. It had been torturing me for over two months now. Today when I didn't come home from work, I wondered if it was wondering where I was at. I kept looking at the hands on the clock. When the clock struck midnight, I opened the bible and began to read Psalms 91' aloud. When I was finished, I sat there looking around the room. I felt as if I weren't alone. I was sure at anytime I would be hit or pushed. I began praying aloud again. I prayed all through the night until daylight.

When mom opened her bedroom door in the morning, I jumped. I still had the bible opened to Psalms 91'. Mom looked at me and said, "did you get any sleep?" I said, "No mom." she told me that I really needed my sleep. I told her that I hadn't slept but two hours a night in that house since I moved in it and I was used to not getting any sleep. I had to start getting ready for work.

When I arrived at work, Allie and I didn't have very many rooms to do so we talked a lot more about what had went on in the house. I even told Allie about me leaving my body and how it tried to keep me from going back in. By the time I got home, the girls were restless because they didn't have any toys to play with. Since mom lived in a basement apartment, she was afraid that the girls were making too much noise for the people that lived above her. She said she was going upstairs to talk to the people and make sure and ask them if the girls were making too much noise. The people upstairs were a young couple with a baby. I knew I could hear them and their baby really good sometimes. When mom came back downstairs, she said that they haven't heard them. She told them if the girls got too noisy to call and let her know and they said they would.

Allie called my moms that evening and asked if I could come over and talk to her mom Katlin. Katlin was real religious and very active in church. I knew Katlin for as long as I knew Allie so I was always comfortable around her. I always liked Katlin, she was a good person. I told Allie I would ask mom if she would watch the girls. Mom said yes. So I got in my van and drove over. Allie lived across the street from her mom. Allie was at her moms when I pulled up. I got out of the van and went over to Katlin's house. When I walked in, Katlin, Allie, and Katlin's ex husband Jeff were sitting there. Kaltin and Jeff remained good friends after they divorced. Allie said, "Cindy, tell mom what you saw and explain to her how you leave your body and what this thing does to you. So I explained the best way I could of what had taken place. When I started telling them about the last time I got beat, I began to cry. I felt stupid. I didn't want to cry in front of them but it was hard enough to try to talk about what this thing did to me. I saw Katlin look at Jeff. My first thought was, oh no, they think I'm crazy but Katlin said, "Cindy, I'll get you some holy water from the church. Just then Jeff spoke up and said, "Forget it Katlin, it won't help. It's going to take a lot more than holy water for this thing." Allie and I started talking. Katlin and Jeff walked to the other side of the kitchen. I was telling Allie that I didn't know what I was going to do because all of the people that were called from churches were too afraid to go in the house. I also told her that the priest I called thought it was a joke. Jeff and Katlin were looking something up in the phone book. Jeff picked up the phone and started dialing. Katlin walked over to me and Allie. She told us that Jeff was calling the head priest in this area. He was in another town close by. Katlin, Allie, and I were having our own conversation while Jeff was conversing with the priest. Jeff had been talking awhile when he walked over to me and told me that the priest wanted to talk to me. When I got on the phone, the priest asked, "Are you on drugs or do you drink alcohol? I replied, "This has nothing to do with alcohol or drugs. Don't you understand this evil thing is trying to kill me? Please help me, if you don't help me I'm going to die!" I started crying so hard that I had to hand the phone back to Jeff. I was so upset. This priest was my last hope. I looked at Allie and said. "He thinks I'm an alcoholic or a drug-addict. Jeff was talking to the priest awhile longer. The priest asked for my mother's phone number. When Jeff hung up, I stayed a little while longer. I finally said that I had better get going; I needed to be with the girls. I was sure with all of their nervous energy that they would be driving mom crazy by now. I said my goodbyes and thanked them for trying to help me. I got in my van and drove off.

 On the way home, I started thinking about the priest. If he didn't believe me then what was I going to do? I started talking to God out loud. I said, "God, you know I'm not crazy. You know exactly what's been going on. If the priest doesn't believe me, ill never get any help. God, I can't fight this thing on my own, l don't even know how. I need the priests help. So please some how make him understand that I need his help." By the time I reached moms, I felt like I was going to lose my mind. I told my mom about the priest. I also told her I didn't think he believed me. It was getting late so everyone went to bed, everyone but me. I stayed up all night reading Psalms 91".

 When daylight came, I started getting ready for work. Work went about the same. When I walked in mom's door she said, "The priest you spoke to last night, Father Anderson, called today." He had asked her some questions about me. He told her that he wanted to talk to me and that he had left a number so I could call him back. I took the number and began punching the numbers on the phone. Father Anderson talked to me for a long time asking me questions. I told him everything I could think of that had taken place in the house. Before we hung up he said he would keep in touch.

The morning I had left the house, I hadn't brought the girls and I many clothes. I had been hand washing what little we had at mom's house. Mom said, "Cindy, I'll go up with you and we can get more clothes. I said, "No mom, I can't go back there, I'm too afraid." She said, well, you can't keep washing and wearing the same clothes day after day. Uncle Randy stopped by later and said he would go up to the house with mom to get some clothes. I really didn't want anyone going into that house and coming back to mom's house. I feared it would follow them. I finally agreed to let them go on one condition. They were both to pray before they entered the house and as they were leaving. They both said that they would. Before they went out the door, mom said that she would bring back some of the girls' dolls. I yelled, "No!" everyone was staring at me. "You can't do that mom, it might get into their dolls and come back with you." I know I sounded crazy but I was terrified of that evil thing.

As soon as mom and Randy walked in the door, the TV went off. I looked at both of them and said; "You didn't pray did you?" everything was quiet. I repeated myself and asked again, "you didn't pray did you?" I was really upset and so were the girls. Mom and Randy both looked at each other and said, "Yes, we prayed." I said, "If you did, why did the TV go off?" They both looked a little scared themselves now. I started praying to myself. That's all I did was pray. Even when I went to work, the bible went with me in the van. I never took it out of the van though. I didn't have to because there was a bible in every room. Mom must have spoken to Taylor earlier that day when I was at work. Taylor called and asked, "Cindy, are you ok?" I replied, "No." I bit my lip to try to keep from crying. She said, "Listen, I spoke to a man over here in Missouri. He gave me a phone number of a psychic, her name is Carrie. She is on your side of the river in Illinois. I want you to call her; the man I spoke to named Kurt said she would help you." I started to cry. I thanked her and hung up the phone. Somebody was going to actually help me, I couldn't believe it. As I was dialing the number I thought, "when I tell her everything she will probably think that I'm crazy." The phone began ringing. I heard a women's voice. I said, "I need to speak with Carrie." She said, "This is Carrie." I said, "My name is Cindy, my sister gave me your number and told me to call you." The first thing that Carrie said was, "Cindy, you're not crazy. What is happening to you is real. I'm sorry but this thing is too powerful for me to go into the house. Its demon like." she said, "I know you are afraid of a fire in the house." I said, "yes I am." She said, "Don't be, this thing is doing this to scare you. It knows if there was a fire then it has no where to go. It would burn with it and it doesn't want that to happen. Now have you had any trouble with your body since you've lived up in that house, from your rib cage up?" I replied, "Yes, my heart." I explained what was taking place every night. She explained that the evil thing was stealing my energy and making itself stronger. The evil thing flashed in my mind, all the energy and strength it held in the middle of that cloud. It all made sense now. Carrie then asked, "do you have a picture of Jesus with a light around him where he is glowing?" I replied, "No I don't." She said, "Get one and study the light around him." Then she asked, "Have you ever looked up in the sky and its really bright like its opening up to heaven?" I said, "Yes." she said, "Picture that light in your mind. When you want to go to sleep, picture yourself laying there and wrap the light all around your body. Start with your toes and bring it up all around your body, cover your head with it." The way Carrie explained it, the light would be my protector. She said to wrap the light around everyone who is in the house with me. That meant my children and my mom. She also told me to keep practicing until I had the light around me all of the time. Then I was to go in the house, get all of my possessions I needed then get the hell out of there and never look back. I was told to put the house up for sale and hire movers to pack everything. She said that they would get everything out for me. I said, "But if I sell the house, what happens to whoever buys it? I wouldn't wish this on my worst enemy. I don't think I could live with myself knowing that some other family would have to go through the same hell we were going through." Carrie said, "Cindy, it lives there and it has always been there. It is attracted to you and as long as your there it will come out. You had better start thinking about Cindy and Cindy's life. If this thing comes out again it may be thirty or fifty years from now. Just remember, as long as you're there, it will stay out." I said, "Carrie, I have been talking to a priest and I am hoping he will help me." She said, " if he can help you then that's great!" Before she hung up, she told me to let her know what happens, I told her I would and I thanked her for helping me understand more of what was going on in the house. After we hung up, I felt a lot better.

Taylor called me and I thanked her for telling Carrie so much. Taylor said, "I didn't even talk to her, I talked to Kurt for a few minutes and he gave me her phone number." Taylor told me that Kurt and Carrie were good Psychics. I was to find out just how good she really was. Before we hung up, I told Taylor thanks again and that I would keep in touch with her and let her know what was going on.

The priest called again. He wanted to know all the names of the doctors I had ever been to and any medications I had been on. He asked me a few more questions. I told him about Carrie and he wasn't too thrilled knowing I had been talking to a psychic. I told him she believed in God and I explained about the light. Before he hung up he said he would keep in touch.

Days turned into weeks. Thanksgiving came and I could have been eating sawdust for all I knew. I was like a walking zombie. People were coming and going all day and all evening at moms. I tried not to talk but everyone was asking questions. I still couldn't speak right so mom spoke for me a lot. By now she knew everything that had went on in the house. Kendra called my moms and wanted to know what was going on? She said she was wondering what was going on because no one was staying at the house not even Jake. She said he would feed the dog and then leave. She also said that Todd had told her some of what was going on and how I couldn't speak right anymore. I said, "Kendra, everything I own is in that house so please watch the house for me. Word is spreading fast in this town about what's going on and everyone knows I'm not staying there." She said, "No problem Cindy." She would tell whoever was watching Brett, to watch my house. I told her I didn't want anyone even near the house other than my Uncle Todd, my mom, or my Uncle Randy, and of course Jake to feed the dog. If anyone else showed up, I told her to call the police. I asked her to keep moms number by her phone and to call if anything should happen.

A few days later, Father Anderson called again. He asked if I was a devil worshiper. I said, "No! I have always believed strongly in God since I was old enough to understand about him." Then he had asked if I had been around anyone that worshiped the devil. I told him not to my knowledge, if I was, I wasn't aware of it. Then he asked, " Have you ever read tarot cards?" I said, "Well yes, just for fun. I have a book on it. I borrowed it from my cousin." He asked me if the book was in the house and I told him that it was. He said that the book had to be removed from the house. "Can you get someone to go in the house and get it?" he asked. I said that I would find someone. When we hung up, I thought to myself, maybe he is going to help me otherwise why would he want the book removed?

Grandma had called my Uncle Nick and told him what was going on. He called to see how I was doing. I told him about my conversation with the priest. He said, "Cindy, I'll come by your moms, get the key and ill go in and get the book." I asked Nick if he was sure he wanted to do that. I asked Nick if he was afraid and he said that he would be alright. He said he was bringing his girlfriend Debra with him. When I hung up, I thanked God for having a family that was standing by me and going to help me. When

Nick came to get the key, his girlfriend and another couple were with him. I hoped they didn't think I was crazy when I said to pray before they went in and before they left. They said they would. When Nick got back, he told me he had put the book in the B.B.Q. pit outside the house. I said, "No, Nick get it away from the house. It belongs to Scott." Scott was my cousin and his nephew. I told Nick to give it to him. I hoped Nick wasn't mad at me because he was already at mom's house when he told me that he put it in the B.B.Q. pit. So that meant they had to go back and get it. I told them that I was sorry and they said it was alright. Before Nick went out the door he said, "Cindy, the guy with me checked the wiring in your box. He said no wonder you were having so much trouble, your wiring is all backwards." I said, "That can't be, I had an electrician fix it. Nick said, "Well, it's all backwards now." I knew this evil thing was smart but I didn't know how smart until Nick told me about the wiring. I thought about what the electrician said, "Someone has purposely turned your wiring around." When things first started going crazy in the house, I remember screaming, "What the hell have I bought?" Now I knew there was no doubt in my mind, I had bought into a piece of hell! I prayed silently, "Please God, let Father Anderson help me." I thought back to our conversation we had about the doctor's numbers. He wanted to talk to them before he spoke to me again. I wondered if he had called and spoke to them and if that's why his attitude has changed about believing me.

I began praying as I always did. Nick had left to go back and get the book. I told him to call when he got back home which was in Cahokia, Illinois. It wasn't that far so I got worried when he didn't call right away. Kendra had called me earlier. She said that my Uncle Nick was up there and had showed her the key and told her why he was up there and she wanted to know how I was doing. She said, "Cindy, I hope you hurry up and get help so you can move back in the house. Brett really misses the girls." I told her that the girls missed Brett also. I paced back in fourth praying. The phone finally rang and it was Nick. His first words were, "You're not going to believe what happened." I asked, "What happened?" He said when he went back to get the book; they started arguing about whether or not to burn the book or give it back to Scott. When they got ready to leave, the door wouldn't open in the van that they were driving. It was Nick's friends van and earlier they had no problem with it. The women got scared and Nick's friend told them that it happens all of the time. Nick said when they reached Cahokia; his friend turned to him and said that he had lied because everyone was so scared. He said that he had never had any trouble with the doors before. When we hung up, I began praying. I still hadn't gotten any sleep and I wondered how much more my body could take.

Taylor came by moms one evening. She had a friend with her and he wanted to see the house. I, myself, had never met her friend but I had seen pictures of him before. He was a professional wrestler, his name was Luke. I felt bad that they had driven all the way from St. Louis but I didn't want them going in the house. I said, "Taylor, just drive by and park on the street, he can see the house from there. What ever you do, don't drive up the hill." I knew ever since we were kids when Taylor was up to something. She had that look in her eyes now. Well I didn't give her a key so the only way she could get in was to break in and I knew that Taylor was smarter than that. Before she went back out the door I said, "I mean it Taylor, don't go up the hill." she said, "Alright Cindy, we won't." About twenty minutes later, I got a call from Kendra. She said, "someone with Missouri license plates was at the house. It was man and a woman. The man was real big and had a bat standing on the porch screaming at the house." I said, "That's my sister and a friend of hers. I told her not to go up the hill." Kendra said, "Well I'm sorry but I called the police. I didn't know who it was. They already left but I gave the police the license plate number." I said, "Kendra, that's ok, you only did what I asked you to do. Everything I own is in that house and I'm just thankful you're watching it for me." Just then someone knocked at the door and I told Kendra I would get back to her. When I opened the door, there stood the policeman that had been sent to my house when Jake was getting his things out. He said, "Cindy, I want to talk to you." I remember thinking, good luck because I can hardly speak. He said, "Ok, do you want to tell me what's going on in that house?" I said, "I don't think you would believe me." He said, "try me." So I explained some of what had been going on in the house. I hoped he could understand everything that I said. He got a call from the dispatcher but he ignored it and kept staring at me. Last time I spoke to him, I could speak as normal as he could. He finally answered the dispatcher. He told me that they had stopped my sister and her friend but they let them go. When he left, I wondered if he thought I was crazy. Kendra called me later. She knew the policeman and she said when he left me he called her and said, "Why the hell did you send me to a damn spook house?" Kendra said he was really shook up. I told her I thought that he thought I was crazy. She said, "No, he believed you."

I still hadn't slept. All I did was pray. Father Anderson called me again. He asked if I had watched any Nightmare on Elm Street movies. That really upset me because I was wondering what he was trying to imply. I said, "Yes Father Anderson I have watched them, hasn't everybody?" At the time, I didn't think much about it but later I could see the similarity, me leaving my body and someone attacking me. I knew that it sounded crazy but with God as my witness, it happened.

Kendra called me that week to tell me that Jake hadn't been by in a few days to feed the dog and she thought I should know. Jake was mad at me because he had called several times trying to get me to come home. This was a way of forcing me to go up to the house. I thanked Kendra for letting me know before I hung up. I told mom about what Kendra said about the dog. Mom said, "Cindy, you can't leave the dog up there on the hill without anything to eat or drink. Tell me where the food is and I will go up there and feed her myself." I said, "No mom, you can't go in there by yourself!" she said, "Then we will go together." I thought about what Carrie had said about the evil thing getting its strength from me. I hadn't been to the house in over a month so it had to be getting weak by now. The food was in the kitchen so all I had to do was get the bucket from outside, fill it with water, and grab some food. I could do that in a matter of minutes. So I agreed to go up with mom. We got in the van and I started driving. I got half way there and almost turned around. I dreaded going up the hill, I wasn't ready for this. I was so scared. Even though it was daylight, I still didn't want to go in the house or anywhere near it. I prayed all the way to the house. When I got on the porch, I let out a scream. Mom said, "Stop it Cindy!" I pointed to the front door. I asked, "What is that?" It was a large crucifix hanging by the front entrance of the door. I said, "Who did this?" Mom said, "Jake probably put it there for protection." Mom told me to give her the key so we could get the dog food. I just wanted to turn around and leave but I didn't. I prayed the whole time I was getting the dogs water. I fed the dog and watered her in record time.

When we got back to moms, she began getting really sick. I felt bad for her because I knew that somehow that evil thing was to blame. I had put her through enough the past month in a half. It was too much on mom. Her apartment was small to begin with. Haley wasn't making anything any easier. Ever since the first night me and the girls moved in with mom, Haley was there also. The girls quit sleeping with mom awhile back because it was getting too hard for her. They would kick and talk in their sleep so mom wasn't getting the proper rest. So every night the girls and Haley were piled on mom's living room floor. Her once immaculate apartment was now a cluttered mess. I still hadn't had any sleep and mom would sit there and look at me with pity in her eyes. All I ever did was hold the bible and pray when I wasn't working. I wasn't like a person at all, more like a robot.

Father Anderson called me again and asked if I would be willing to undergo a psychological evaluation. I said, "Yes, I will even take a lie detector test. Anything so you will believe me." He said all that wouldn't be necessary. He said he would set up an appointment and I said that I would be there. When I hung up the phone, I told mom what was going on. I told her that it wouldn't be long before she could have her house back to herself. I called Jake at his moms and he was elated. My happy high turned low by evening. I kept thinking what if I didn't pass the evaluation? What if he said I was crazy? Then I would think of things that had happened, "No, I'm not crazy." I prayed all night and asked God to once again give me the strength I needed to get through this.

 The appointment was set up and now it was time for me to go. I was so afraid. I had never been through anything like this before. I wondered what all was about to take place. I prayed all the way to the doctors office, "Please God, don't let this doctor think I'm crazy!" By now, I was beginning to doubt my own sanity. When we pulled up to park the van, mom asked, "Are you ready to go in?" I said, "As ready as ill ever be." We walked in and I gave the receptionist my name and I told her I was here to see Dr. Morgan. When I sat down, mom looked at me and said, "It will be ok, you will do fine Cindy." a door opened and my name was called. I felt like a little girl again. I didn't want to go in there alone; I wanted my mother to come with me. Mom always made things better when I was small but I wasn't a little girl and I had to do this on my own. Dr. Morgan introduced himself and shut the door. The questions began and I began answering them. Then he asked, "have you always studdered?" I said no that it started the day I left the house. We talked for a long time about everything that took place in the house. Everything came out, even about my dreams. Since I was very young I would dream things and they would happen. I told him one particular dream I had when I was pregnant with Sydney. I actually witnessed a murder before it occurred. I watched a women being tortured and raped by several men. I could feel the pain and I assumed it was me only with long hair, I never saw the woman's face. I had never seen so much blood in my life. There are more details of the murder that I wont mention, it was horrible. When I woke up there were skulls all over the room. Some had hair on them and some had lit candles in their mouths. They were clicking their jaws up and down. I was staying at my moms at the time and I had been sleeping on a chair bed. I crawled over to the light to turn it on. These things were so noisy. As soon as I hit the switch, they disappeared. My heart was beating so fast I could see my shirt rising up and down. I thought for sure I would lose the baby. I went in my mom's room and woke her up to tell her what had happened. The next day my sister called and said, "Cindy, are you sitting down?" I said, "No why?" she said, "I think you better." I said, "Taylor what is wrong? What happened Taylor, tell me." She began telling me that someone I knew had been raped and murdered by several men. That woman could have been Sydney's aunt if she would have lived. It was her beautiful hair I had seen. I told Taylor that I had woke mom up about 3:00am that morning because I had a dream about it. I was there and it was something I would never forget for as long as I lived.. It was the worst thing I have ever seen in my life. Taylor said it had happened a few hours after I had dreamed it. I told Taylor that I was sick to my stomach and I had to hang up. I went into more detail with Dr. Morgan about what had happened to her. Since it was in all the newspapers he said that he remembered it well. Dr. Morgan then asked, "Did you tell Father Anderson about how you dream things and they happen." I said, "No, I didn't think that was important." "What about being in contact with spirits since you were small?" I replied, "No, I didn't." We talked a little more. I said, "Dr. Morgan, I know what I've told you sounds crazy, about the evil thing beating me and the people coming out of the wall. I'm not crazy Dr. Morgan; I swear everything I told you was true." I was sitting there looking at Dr. Morgan, he held all the cards. Right now my whole life was in his hands. He could either make me or break me for good. Dr. Morgan looked me straight in the eyes and said, "Cindy, the only thing wrong with you is that you have too much psychic ability." I felt fresh tears flowing down my cheeks. When I calmed down, Dr. Morgan told me that he was going to contact Father Anderson. Dr. Morgan asked me, " What exactly do you want him to do?" I said, "Whatever it takes to get the evil thing out of my house so I can have my life back, that's all I ever wanted." Our session was now over and I thanked Dr. Morgan. When I walked into the waiting area, I walked over to where my mom was sitting. I said, "Mom, I'm not crazy." I began to cry again. Mom hugged me with tears in her own eyes. She said, "I told you, you would do ok." I was glad that this part of my living nightmare was over. Word spread fast in our small town. The ones who looked at me as if I were crazy, now looked at me a little differently. I didn't really care what anyone thought about me anymore. I just wanted to be normal again and be able to speak right and live. I wasn't really living at all; I was more like a robot. I didn't want to be afraid anymore.

  Father Anderson called me again and asked me to go and get copies of all the deeds of anyone who had ever lived in that house. I told him that I would go and get the deeds. I hadn't spoken to Jake since I had passed the evaluation, he even believed me now. I was still scared of him though. I really didn't want to be around him. He had said things that really hurt me and that I would never forget. He accused me of making all this up in the beginning. The reason being was because I hated the house so much. Id say, "Jake, you've known me for ten years and you know better. I couldn't make something like that up. I've never lied to you before, why should I start now? I don't even think someone with a brilliant imagination could have made something like this up. I don't give a damn how much I hated the house; I wouldn't just walk out and leave everything I own to be cramped up in a one bedroom apartment! What about my mom and the children? Don't you think this is tearing them apart? Do you think I would deliberately disrupt everyone's lives this way? No Jake, that's not me and you know it. Listen to me, I can't even speak right anymore. Jake, have you ever been so frightened that you couldn't speak? Well take a good long look at me because that is what has happened to me. Jake I don't care if you believe me or not. Just be careful when you're in that house." Jake said, "I don't know what to believe anymore." Now a month later he was standing here telling me he believed me the whole time. I knew that Jake hadn't slept in the house since I had been gone. He had been staying at his moms the whole time. He only went up to feed the dog. I remembered the times he didn't feed the dog and I wondered if something had happened to him and he just wasn't telling me. Jake must have been afraid of something or he wouldn't have hung a crucifix on the wall.

Jake missed the girls as much as they missed Jake. I agreed to try one more time with him when the priest got the evil thing out of the house; which I told him would be real soon. All I had to do now was to get the deeds. A few days later, I got the copies of all the deeds. Days went by and I still hadn't heard from him. In the mean time, things were still the same. I was still scared all the time and I always had the bible in my hands and I still hadn't slept. The hotel business was slow so I didn't get very many hours. I knew I was getting on my moms nerves. All I did was pray.

One day mom talked me into going to the clinic because I hadn't had a pap smear for awhile. She was going to get one too so I agreed to go. I didn't want to be by myself anyway, I was too paranoid to stay alone. When we arrived, they called me in first. They took a pap smear and then a urine sample. The nurse asked me to wait in the waiting room for my results. Another nurse called my mom in for a pap smear. A nurse came back to the waiting room and said, "Cindy, I need to speak with you for a minute." I followed her down the hall and into a room. She told me to have a seat. I sat down and she began talking. She said, "the urine test we took show that you have traces of blood in your kidneys." I sat there thinking, "Blood in my kidneys?" I remembered my last beating being kicked in the kidneys so hard I thought I was going to die. The nurse was saying something but my mind was on my last beating. I said, "I'm sorry, what did you say?" she said, "I asked if you have a regular physician?" I answered, "Yes." She said,

"I want you to make an appointment as soon as possible." I wanted to tell her that I knew exactly what was wrong. I had just been to my physician not long before and he ran the same test. My urine was clear then. I took my worst beating after he had run the test. I told the nurse that I would make an appointment. When I walked out of the room, I knew I wouldn't call my doctor. Why should I spend more money when I knew damn good and well how the blood had gotten there? I walked down the hall and back in the waiting room. Mom was sitting there reading a book. She said that she was all through and asked if I was ready to go. I said, "Yes." Then I said, "Mom, I have blood in my kidneys." She said, "What!" I repeated myself and told her it was from the last beating. I said, "Mom, he left his mark this time. Now I have all the proof I need."

Christmas was right around the corner. Christmas had always been my favorite holiday. I had animated figurines and a lot of decorations. Mom had started a tradition when I was very young, cookie baking. We would bake dozens of cookies of all types. Everyone would come over to moms for cookies. We would give our best friends cookies also. Mom had always decorated her house up really nice. The girls always enjoyed looking at all her beautiful decorations. The previous year, I had bought a lot of new things at the end of the season. Not long after we moved into the house, the girls and I were discussing where we were going to put up the Christmas tree and all of our new decorations. We had decided on the TV room downstairs. The girls were so excited, I remember saying, "Well Christmas will be here before we know it and it will be the best Christmas ever." As I sat there thinking about it, it seemed so unfair. All our beautiful decorations were locked up in the house being held prisoner with the evil being. I knew I had gifts to buy but I really didn't want to go shopping but for the sake of my loved ones, I knew I had to. I really couldn't tell you how I made it through the Christmas shopping that year.

About a week before Christmas, some of my cousins stopped by to see how I was doing. One of them was Alex. By now I looked like the walking dead, I still had not slept for even one minute. Someone asked me why I hadn't tried to get any sleep. I said that I was too scared. I said, "I know it knows I'm here and if I fall asleep, I will leave my body and I know I will get beat and I don't think my body could handle another beating." Strange things had happened at moms ever since Randy and mom went up to that house. Her kitchen light had gone on by itself one night. The vaporizer she had plugged in when she was sick had blown up and a few times we had blown fuses. Besides, I could feel something around me a lot of the time. More than once I felt my heart skip beats. I knew for a fact that my mom had spirits in her house because I had seen them with my own two eyes but they were not evil ones. I had never ever come in contact with an evil one until I moved into my house. Since I always had the bible right next to me, when I would feel something by me, I would always read Psalms 91" and it always helped me. I was sitting there in my own little world when Alex said something that put chills up my spine. He said, "Cindy I know you are afraid of this thing finding you but have you ever thought about you leaving your body and going back up to the house?" That was something I hadn't thought about. I had enough fear consummating my life. Now I had one more thing to be fearful of. I wished that Alex wouldn't have brought this matter to my attention. My biggest fear had been since this evil thing was so smart that it was sitting back waiting for me to fall asleep so it could attack me. I knew that someday soon I would have to get some sleep because I knew my body was wearing down. But I would keep fighting sleep for as long as I had any fight left in me.

That night after everyone had left; mom and the girls went to sleep. I prayed to God to please give me the strength to stay awake until Father Anderson gets the evil thing out of my life. I guess I didn't have to worry about going to sleep because I was so afraid. I don't think I could have slept if I wanted to. Sometimes I felt so tired but all I had to do was to think of the evil being and my tiredness would pass quickly. Since I had done everything Father Anderson had asked me to do, I wondered why he hadn't done anything yet.

One night Uncle Randy stopped by mom's house. It was late and when I heard the knock at the door, I think I had jumped a foot. Randy said he had just dropped Jennifer off at her trailer and on the way back, he had driven by the house. Then he asked, "Cindy, were you up at the house tonight?" I said, "Hell no, are you kidding?" He said, "I didn't think so. Well is Jake up there?" I said, "No, Jake doesn't stay at the house and besides he is working." Randy said, "Well, your house is lit up like a Christmas tree." Mom and I said, "What!" at the same time. He said, "Every light in your house is on, you can see it real good from the street." Randy said, "Why don't you and your mom drive by and look?" I said no that I didn't want to. Randy said, "you don't have to go up the hill, just drive by on the street, I want you to see this." Mom was all for going so I finally agreed to go. Only I didn't drive all the way past the house, I got part way there and started to get scared. I drove a little further and just like Randy had said, the house was lit up like a Christmas tree.

When Christmas was near, the girls said, "Mom, it doesn't even seem like Christmas this year, you're always praying and scared. You don't even act like yourself." Sydney said, "I wish we could go and get our decorations from our house. I said a little too sharply, "well we can't Sydney! Don't even think about it!" The minute I yelled at Sydney I was sorry. I apologized to both girls for yelling at them and for the way I had been acting. I told them as soon as the priest helps me that I would be ok again. I said, "As for the decorations, grandma has just as many beautiful things as we have. Just hang in there with me girls, all this will be over soon, I promise. Then everything will be back to normal again."

On Christmas, a lot of my aunts, uncles, and cousins came by. Mom had gone ahead and baked lots of cookies just like she had every year. My cousins drove by the house to see if anything was going on. They ended up parking on the street and watched the house. They saw something in the window. Jake called and asked me if he could spend the night since it was Christmas Eve. The girls still believed in Santa and he wanted to be there when they woke up in the morning to open their gifts. I told him I would ask mom and call him back.

His dad had gotten really sick; he had to be operated on. He was diagnosed with cancer. After he was released from the hospital, he was put in a nursing home. I went to see him a few times and it broke my heart. Each time I saw him he told me that he didn't belong there. Jake and I told him that we would find a way to get him out. Jake and I went to see him Christmas Eve and we promised him we would be back early in the morning and we would take him home. I knew Jake's mom would be mad if she knew what we were up to. I loved Jake's dad, he was a good man. He took up for me more than once when Jake and I were fighting. He needed me now and I didn't care who got mad. I was going to take him home Christmas day.

Mom said Jake could spend the night. Jake and I slept on the floor with the girls. When everyone was asleep, we put all the gifts under the tree. When we were through, we laid back down. I held the bible and watched the lights on the Christmas tree blinking off and on. When I heard Jake snoring, I started to pray. I prayed to myself until daylight as I always did. When the girls woke up, they were excited. When the girls started opening their gifts, I was just as surprised as they were of what they were opening. I knew I had bought the gifts but I didn't even remember what I had bought. Lindsey wanted a Pamela doll; I knew I had bought that. When Lindsey saw it, she was so happy. I said, "Wait a minute Lindsey, in order for her to talk, you have to put the disc in her. Lindsey picked her up and she began talking. Lindsey threw the doll across the room and began screaming and crying. Mom picked the doll up. We checked the doll. There was already a disc built inside of her that we hadn't known about. I tried to explain to Lindsey but it was too late, I had already ruined everything for her. She didn't want anything to do with the doll. I couldn't remember anything that I bought for my relatives that year. I do remember Jake handing me a velvet pouch. I opened it up. It was an expensive gold chain. Any other time, I would have been thrilled but it just didn't seem like Christmas to me. Jake had a hurt look on his face when he asked, "What's wrong Cindy? Don't you like it?" I said, "I'm sorry Jake, I love it. It's beautiful. It just doesn't seem like Christmas to me." Then I thought of someone else. Maybe I wasn't happy but I knew someone that I could make happy today. I said, "Come on Jake, lets go get your dad." We got ready and went to the nursing home. Jake's dad was waiting when we arrived. We drove up Jake's mom and dad's hill. He drove straight to the back door, his dad was pretty weak. I explained to Jake's dad that I had relatives coming over to moms and that I would be back later. Jake's dad said, "Merry Christmas Cindy." I saw the tears of joy in his eyes. I felt my eyes watering up too. When I drove away I was crying for Jake's dad.

When I got back to moms, I took my bath and put my makeup on. I tried to look the best I could. Our relatives would be arriving soon. Haley was already there when Taylor and Tyler arrived. We were sitting there talking when the telephone rang. Mom handed me the phone. I said, "Hello." It was Allie. She asked, "Cindy, who is all over at your house?"

I said, "Well, me, mom, Taylor... she interrupted me and said, "No at your house." I said, "no one." Allie said, "yes there is, we just drove up there and a man was standing in the upstairs window." I said, "Allie if someone was at my house, Kendra would have called me. I'm going to hang up Allie and call Kendra, thanks for calling me." I dialed her number and the phone rang and rang. I said, "damn" aloud. Taylor said, "what's wrong?" I explained what Allie had told me. I said I guessed that Kendra and Brett had gone to her mom's house for Christmas. I just hope no one is robbing me blind. Taylor said, "Come on, lets go see what's going on." I said, "Taylor, I really don't want to go over there. Taylor said, "Let's just go see if the door is open then." I said, "Alright, "let's go. I prayed all the way over to the house. Taylor and I got out of the car together and we walked up to the door. I turned the knob and it was locked. She told me to unlock the door very quietly so we could see who was in there. I did as Taylor asked. We looked around and nothing had been disturbed. We crept up the stairs and nothing was up there either. All at once I knew exactly who was at the window. I said, "Oh, shit! Taylor come on, we need to get out of here." Taylor looked at me as if I were crazy and asked, "what's going on?" I said, "Taylor, the only one here is the one who has always been here. We were tricked. Now let's go." On the way home I kept praying, "Please God don't let it follow us."

Not long after Christmas, my uncle Todd called. He said he and his wife would like me to come to church with them the following Sunday. He said the girls and I would really enjoy it. I said that I would talk to the girls about it and call him back. I talked it over with the girls and they wanted to go. I called Todd back and told him that we decided to go. He said he would come by and pick us up Sunday morning. I told him thanks and that we would see him Sunday morning. The only problem I had with going was that I didn't have a dress at mom's house. I hadn't been called into work lately and I wondered why? I know when I was at work, strange things would happen. Things that not scared only me but Allie too. For instance, Allie and I would be walking down the hall and the lights would start flickering. Another time, Allie and I walked into a room and the bible was laying wide open. A lot of strange things were happening at work. Since I hadn't been working, I couldn't afford to run out and buy a new dress. I had no choice but to go up to the house and get one. I thought about sending someone else up there but I would need to get my dress shoes, earrings, and a few other things. I dreaded going up to that house. At first, I told myself that I had several days until Sunday so I had put off going. Time was running out, I only had two days left.

When Nick called to see how I was doing, I told him that I was supposed to go to church and explained about the dress and other things I needed to get. He said, "Cindy, hold on for a minute." He got back on and said, "Me and Debra will come by tomorrow and take you up to the house." I told him thanks and hung up. I thought it would be safer with the three of us going. I still dreaded going because I had to go upstairs to get the things I needed. It wasn't as if I could walk upstairs and back out. I would have to take time to look for what I needed.

Later that evening, Father Anderson called me. He asked how I was doing. I said, "Not good, I still haven't had any sleep. I told him I was going to church Sunday morning with my uncle, his wife, and my kids. I told him that they were very religious people. He said that he was glad that I was going. I explained to him about the dress and other stuff I had to get from the house. I told him how I was dreading going up to the house when my Uncle Nick called and said he would take me up to the house. Father Anderson said, "Cindy, be careful. By now the evil knows you're trying to get away from it, so it is really mad now. If the little boy appears while you are in the house, do not speak to him, turn around and go straight out the door. Ignore him and leave the house." I said, "But I'm not afraid of the little boy." Father Anderson asked, "Did you hear what I said?" Father Anderson sounded upset with me just because I said I wasn't afraid of the little boy. I said, "Yes, I heard you but I don't feel any evil with the little boy so I'm not afraid of him. Father Anderson was really upset now as he said in a stern voice, "Cindy, listen to me, the little boy and the evil are the same." That really threw me. I was scared of the man, the old woman, and I was petrified of the evil pinkish cloud of energy, But the boy, he was so different or so I thought. He looked so much like my nephew Tyler, maybe that's what threw me off. I remembered a previous conversation that Father Anderson and I had. He had asked me if the boy looked like anyone I knew. At first I had hesitated. I was afraid to say that he looked like my nephew Tyler for the fear that he would think I was crazy. I had taken the risk and told him the truth and now he was telling me that the little boy and the evil were the same. I told father Anderson that I was sorry and that if the little boy appeared that I would leave immediately. I said, "Father Anderson, I thought after the psychological evaluation that you would go in and get the evil out." he said, "I'm working on it. There are things that I have to do before I can go into the house." I said, "Well I have waited this long, I guess I can wait a little longer. Before we hung up he said, "Just remember what I told you and be careful." When we hung up, I thought about the little boy. It was hard for me to believe he was evil but Father Anderson knew more about evil than I did, so I believed him.

The girls were getting on my nerves a lot lately and tonight was no different. I would be glad when Sunday got here. Maybe we would feel better after going to church. Tonight was no different than the rest of the nights, I prayed myself into the daylight. The next day, I waited for Nick and Debra. When they arrived, I told them they could take my van. We got in the van and I began driving. We got half way down mom's hill when I realized that I didn't have any brakes. I said, "Oh God, I can't stop!" I tried pumping them but I still had nothing. The van kept right on going. Thank God there were no cars coming. Nick said, "Cindy, turn around, well take my car." When I checked again, I now had breaks. I said, "Forget it Nick" and I kept driving. When we got there, I prayed to myself. I unlocked the door and we went inside. I looked at Nick and Debra and said, "Let's go." Nick said that he would go first, Debra and I followed. I looked up as we were climbing the stairs and there looking at me was the picture of Jesus. I was surprised to see that it was still hanging. I thought the evil thing would have destroyed it by now. We went into the bedroom and got everything I needed. We were still upstairs when Nick asked,"Which wall did you see the people and the evil come out of?" We were in the upstairs living room so I walked over to the wall and pointed to it. I was a nervous wreck standing there. Nick asked, "do you know where this wall leads downstairs? What room?" I replied, "No, I hadn't really thought about it." He said, "I want to see something." He looked at

Debra and I and said, "You and Debra stand right here and when I yell, I want you to knock on the wall. Nick went downstairs. We heard him yell, so we knocked. He yelled, "Knock harder!" So we did. Nick came back upstairs and said, "The people and the evil thing are coming from your furnace room; Cindy, their coming from underground straight up to where your furnace is." That's also the utility room and toy room. That's where the kids would play and the lights kept going dim and then bright. I bet I had blown about a hundred light bulbs in that room alone. I started getting a bad feeling. I said, "Come on, lets go." We went downstairs. We were in the kitchen when Nick and Debra asked, "What's that smell?" I sniffed and said, "Yuck!" since no one had been living in the house for months, Nick said, "Maybe its something spoiled in the refrigerator." He checked everything in it. Nick said, "I can't figure it out, nothing smells in here at all." I walked to the other side of the room; the odor seemed to be getting stronger. I walked back by Debra and she looked at Nick and said, "Its following Cindy." It was so close to me that I was getting nauseous. I looked over at Nick and Debra and said; "I got to get out of here, I'm sick." My stomach was empty except for the tea that I had drank earlier. As soon as I got outside, I was throwing up. The next thing I knew, I was down on the ground. I tried to get up but something was holding me down. I shouted, "God please help me!" Now I was being choked. I would rise up to try to get away but I would be pulled right back down. Every time I would try to get away, I would be choked even more. I heard the door shut and as I was being choked, I looked up to see Nick and Debra standing there looking at me. I was pleading with my eyes for them to help me. I remember thinking what's wrong with them? Why won't they help me? I tried harder to get away. I kept trying to say, "Help me!" But I kept being knocked down and choked. Nick and Debra were just standing there as if they couldn't move. Maybe they were in shock. Suddenly I heard a loud roar and I screamed, "Help me! Help me!" Nick and Debra picked me up and threw me in the van. My body went limp. Nick flew down the hill. I was crying so hard I could hardly speak. My throat hurt so bad that it was hard to talk when the words came out, it sounded hoarse. Debra was trying to comfort me. She kept saying, "Its ok, its ok Cindy." I asked, "Did you hear it?" I saw Debra and Nick look at each other. I asked again, "Did you hear it?" Debra looked at me and said, "Yes we heard it." I said, "It sounded like it came out of me. Oh God, don't let this thing be in me." Nick said, "we are going over to Todd's house. I can't let your mom and the girls see you this way."

When we got to Todd's house I said, "I don't want to go in." I was still crying and I didn't want anyone to see me. Nick went in and spoke to Todd and his wife Julie. They both came out to the van. They told me that the bad smell was the evil. I told them how it was choking me. They wanted me to go in but all I wanted to do was to go to moms. I wanted to be with mom and my daughters. When I had calmed down enough, Nick and Debra took me back to moms. When I got out of the van, I felt something wet. I looked down at my pants and they were soaked. I hadn't even realized it but when I was being choked, I had urniated..

When I walked into moms, I must have looked a mess. My eyes were almost swollen shut and my pants were soaking wet. Mom looked at me and asked "What happened?" I knew if I answered her that I would start crying again so I ran to the bathroom and let Nick and Debra explain what had happened. I took my wet clothing off and got in the bathtub. The hot water felt so good on my aching body. When I got out of the tub, I got myself together. I picked up the phone to call the psychic Carrie. She answered the phone. I explained everything that had taken place earlier at the house. She said, "The roar did not come out of you, the evil was so close to you, it wanted to make you think that it was in you." I said, "Thank God! I thought it some how had gotten in me." I thanked her for talking to me and we hung up. I sat there thinking of what the evil thing had done to me. When Nick had come upstairs from knocking on the wall, I remembered saying, "I can't wait for the priest to come up here and get the evil thing out of this house." After I had said that, I remember thinking, "I hope its not listening." I wondered if it had heard me or if Nicks knocking on the wall had disturbed it. Maybe it was just mad like the priest had warned me. For whatever reason, it was mad and even though there was no manifestation, it let Nick and Debra know it was there by its smell. It was also mad enough to hold me down and choke me half to death in front of them. I knew one thing; I would not enter that house again until Father Anderson got it out. I wanted him to send it back to hell where it belonged.

I prayed all night until finally it was daylight. Since I was already up, I started to get ready for church. When the girls got up, I got them ready. I asked mom if she wanted to go with us and she said no. She wasn't feeling well and besides she wanted to enjoy the peace and quiet while she could. After all, I walked around like a robot and the girls were restless in her apartment.

Todd, Julie, and their two daughters were right on time to pick us up. It was a long ride to their church. It wasn't near our town. I was surprised the girls were being so quiet. When we finally arrived, I was glad to get out of their vehicle and stretch my legs. When we entered the church, I felt all eyes on us. I knew Todd had spoken to the people about what was going on. The preacher was really good, I liked him right off. When everybody started to sing, the girls and I sang with them. After services, I was feeling better until a man approached me and said, "You need to go back in the house and show this evil thing that it is not going to run you out of your own home." I looked at him and said, "You don't understand, this thing is powerful. I will never go back to the house until the priest gets it out." He kept on me about how I should go back by myself. While he kept talking I stood there listening. I said, "look, you have no idea how powerful this evil thing is. It beats me and it tried to choke me to death! It has tried to kill me more than once and you're telling me to go in there by myself!" I stood there wondering why he didn't offer to go in the house himself. I thought to myself, "God what am I doing here? These people have no idea what I've been going through and I'm standing here arguing with someone I don't even know. I said a silent prayer, "God please let someone understand what's going on and help me, Amen." A woman walked over to me and began talking. After awhile, I began to feel better. She said, "Cindy, we want to pray over you." I said, "Ok." Todd walked over to me and it was as if he read my mind and said, "the girls will be fine, they are with us. You go on with her and get prayed for."

The woman led me over to a room where other people were waiting for us. When we entered the room, someone closed the door. The woman told me to sit down in a chair. The people began praying, they were talking in tongues. At first I didn't know what to think, I was scared. The more they prayed, the more relaxed I became. I know I was prayed over for more than two hours. When they were through praying, someone opened the door. I told them thanks for praying over me. When I stood up, I began stumbling around. Someone said, "Your drunk Cindy, drunk in the spirit." I was lightheaded and so dizzy that I had run into a wall. The girls saw me and came running to ask if I was alright. I said that I was fine. I felt lighter, as if a huge weight had been lifted off me. Hours before, I had asked God what I was doing there. Now I knew and I felt much better. On our way to moms, I told Todd and Julie that I really liked their church. When we got to moms, I thanked them for taking me and the girls. I told them that I was sorry that I was in the room so long. They said it was ok, they were just glad that I was feeling better.

When we walked in, mom had supper waiting. I told her all about the church and what had went on. Mom said, "Cindy, you look so tired, why don't you go lay down in my room for awhile." I said, "Mom, you know I don't want to go to sleep." She said, "Just lie on the bed and relax. Ill keep the girls in here with me." I said, "Alright mom." It had been a long time since I had laid down on a bed. I had began asking God why? As I had asked so many times in the past months. "Why is this happening to me? I just don't understand, why me God?" I opened the bible and began reading; He that dwelleth in the secret place....I could not keep my eyes open. I didn't leave my body but I was in a deep sleep. I found myself standing on a hill. A hill that was all too familiar to me. It was the hill behind my house. I smelled freshly dug dirt. When I looked down at where my house should have been, it was no longer there. What I did see, frightened me. There were a group of men in a circle. They were all dressed in black hooded robes. There was some kind of ritual going on. The men were down on their knees with their arms raised over their heads. Their arms were rising up and down. They were worshiping whatever was in the middle of the circle. They were chanting. I wanted to get a closer look. I was afraid, I knew I couldn't let the men see me. I was still on the hill but the smell of freshly dug dirt filled my nostrils. I was close now. I could see the side view of one mans face. I was now standing next to the man. It was strange, I could see them but they couldn't see me. These men dug what looked like a grave and in the middle was a large wooden crate. The lid was closed but I knew without even looking inside that the crate contained a dead body. I thought to myself, "What are they doing and where did my house go?" All at once, I was lying on the bed with the bible across my chest. I laid there a few minutes trying to collect my thoughts. Had I really been sleeping or had I just left my body without realizing it? It sure seemed more real then just a dream. But if I had left my body, then I had somehow traveled back in time. Then I remembered when I had left my body in my house, I had still been in the house but my kitchen was a laboratory. I wondered, was it possible to somehow travel back in time? It all seemed so crazy.

I told mom what I had seen then I picked up the phone to call Carrie. I explained everything to her. She asked, "have you been asking God why this has been happening to you?" I answered, "Yes." She said, "well, he just showed you why. There is someone buried under your house. Actually there is more than one person buried under there. You also have more spirits in the house than you think." I told her I appreciated all of her help. She said to make sure that I let her know if the priest was going to help me. I said that I would let her know. When I hung up the phone, I thought about what Carrie had said about there being more spirits in there than I thought. I had seen the boy, the man, the old woman, and the pinkish cloud. That was four. I didn't even want to know how many more were living in the house. I thought about the men in the black hooded robes. Were they devil worshipers? Had they murdered people then buried them out in secluded areas years and years ago when there were no houses, just woods? When I was younger, my aunt told me a little bit about devil worshipers. I couldn't understand it then and I don't understand it now. How someone could choose the devil over God and hell over heaven?

I was sitting there praying to myself when the phone rang. I picked it up and said, "Hello?" it was Father Anderson. He said that he needed to talk to me before we could go into the house. I was silent for a moment. We? Father Anderson couldn't possibly mean him and me? He was saying something when I said, "Father I don't want to go in that house, please don't ask me to do that. I could just meet you somewhere and give you the key." He said, "Cindy, you have to be in there with me." I said, "Please don't make me go, I'm too scared!" He then asked, "do you believe that God is stronger than evil?" I answered him, "Yes." He said, "Then you shouldn't be afraid." I said, "Well, I'm still afraid." He said, " I can't help you if you don't cooperate with me." Up until now, I had done everything that Father Anderson asked of me but asking me to go into the house with him was a little too much. Before Father Anderson hung up he said, " I want you to repeat over and over that God is stronger than evil. I will get in touch with you soon." If I said it once, I said it a thousand times. I was still afraid. I was really worried about how the evil would react to me bringing a priest in the house. The priest had even said to me that he didn't know what he would be walking into. I hated the idea of me walking in the house with Father Anderson but I also knew that if I wanted my life back I had no choice in the matter.

For the next week, I prayed even harder than before and I kept repeating that God was stronger than evil. Father Anderson called and asked if I was ready to go into the house. I said that I was as ready as I would ever be. All this time I had never actually met Father Anderson, we had only spoken on the phone. He told me we were to meet at the Catholic Church in my hometown. He told me which day and gave me a time. Then he said, "I want your mother, grandmother, and your two daughters with you." I asked, "What about Jake? He will be living in the house also. He said, "No Cindy, this has to do with your psychic ability and the generations that have psychic ability. I said, "I don't think my grandma can come, she is sick." He said that if she was that sick then she didn't have to come. When I hung up, I was a nervous wreck. I told mom what he had said and she said that she would go.

The day finally arrived. I had prayed all night. I still hadn't slept since the day I had went to the church. I kept thinking about the house. I wondered after everything that had happened if I would be able to even sleep in that house at all. The girls and I had all our things packed to take home. We had accumulated a lot since we had been living at moms. Most of it was from Christmas. We decided to wait until the priest got the evil out, then we would come back and get everything Instead of loading the van up now. We were ready to go. We got in the van and I started driving. I kept saying to myself that God was stronger than evil. I was still scared. I prayed silently for God to keep us all safe. I got to the church and I drove around a few minutes. I parked the van and we began getting out. I told mom that I was afraid. The girls said they were afraid also. I asked mom if she was afraid and she said, "No." Father Anderson introduced himself; he had another priest with him. He introduced him and said he would be going to the house with us. I can't remember exactly what took place in the church. I remember candles being lit and all of us praying. I also remember us taking an oath against evil. Before we had left the church, the priest put holy water on each of us, we prayed again. Father Anderson picked up the bible again and put it in his hands. The bible was wide open. As he held it, I noticed that his hands were trembling. I felt sorry for him. Just because he was a man of God didn't mean he didn't also have feelings. I knew right then that he was as frightened as I was. I looked over at the other priest and he seemed to be calm. I noticed him studying Father Anderson. I didn't ask right then but I wondered if this was the first time Father Anderson had ever done anything like this before. After praying, he told me to go and get my vehicle and pull it around to the front and he and the other priest would follow us to the house.

 I prayed in my mind all the way up to the house and I kept saying that God was stronger than evil. We parked our vehicles and got out. My hand was shaking as I tried to get the key in the lock. I wanted to run and keep on running and never look back. I knew I couldn't., I've come this far. I just prayed that God wouldn't let anything happen to the priest or us. I finally got the key in the door and when we entered the house, there was no sign of the evil. It was really strange. If I didn't know better, I would say that it was just a regular house. Father Anderson opened the bible and held it in both hands and began praying. If his hands were shaking at the church, they were shaking worse now. When he was through praying, he told mom and the girls to stay in the kitchen by the front door. I was to follow in back of the priest. They began going through the house throwing holy water on the walls and saying "Jesus be with us." They threw holy water on the walls of every room in the house. When they were through, the priest said something about our dog. Father Anderson started walking outside over to our dog. The other priest asked if Sydney was the one that the evil spoke through. I said no that it was the youngest one, Lindsey. He had a strange look on his face. When he started to walk off I said, "Excuse me, Father Anderson didn't mention anything about you before. I'm just curious as to why you are with him today." he said that he was from St.

Louis, Mo. He was called to help Father Anderson because he had never experienced anything like this before. So father Anderson had been talking to him all this time. I smiled at the priest and said, "I kind of thought so." When they were through blessing the dog with holy water, I told them thanks for all their help.

Me, mom, and the girls already made plans to go out to eat to celebrate. Something didn't seem right to me though. For one thing, there was no sign of the evil thing at all while the priest was throwing holy water and praying. Secondly, I knew being weak had nothing to do with it. I had stayed away all that time and when I came to get my dress for church, it had the strength to hold me down and near choke me to death. And third, it was too easy. I took mom and the girls to eat and I pretended to be just as happy as they were. But I still had that doubt in the back of my mind. Mom and the girls seemed so happy so I decided to keep my thoughts to myself. Maybe I was wrong after all. Thinking I was wrong really put me in a good mood.

After we finished eating, we drove over to moms to take her home. We loaded up the van. We didn't have room for everything so I told mom that we would be back tomorrow to get the rest of the things. She said that it was fine with her. We kissed and hugged. Before I left, I told her I was sorry that we had to stay with her so long. I knew how hard all this had been on her. I told her that I loved her and she said the same. I promised to call her later. I wouldn't have to worry about the phone anymore either. Since the evil thing was gone, the phone should be working all of the time. When we were leaving, I saw the relief on my moms face. I didn't blame her, the girls were a handful and she deserved her apartment back to herself again. Jake was supposed to meet us over at the house in an hour.

When we arrived at the house, we started unloading our belongings. Everything still looked the same in the house. I think that I expected the house to be torn up. But it looked like any normal house. I thought to myself, "Oh good I was wrong, the priest did get it out." After we put our belongings away, I sat down at the kitchen table. The girls were in the utility room checking out their toys they hadn't seen in months. I was still sitting at the kitchen table when I felt the hair rise on my neck. I thought, "Oh no, it can't be." I said to myself, "Cindy you are just nervous. If the priest thought that he didn't get it out, then he would have told me." I sat there for a few more minutes. I don't remember why I got up and went upstairs but I did. It was then that I realized this was more than just a bad case of nerves. I felt its presence all around me, my ears started closing up. I vaguely heard the girls. I turned around and they were in back of me. They both looked so happy. What was I going to do? I decided not to say anything to the girls. I went back downstairs and sat at the kitchen table. I decided that I would just ignore this evil thing. That's what I was thinking when I heard Sydney screaming, "Mommy its still here, help me!" I ran over to the stairs. The thing had a hold of Sydney, It held her up so she couldn't get down the stairs. I guess I was more mad then scared as I ran towards her. All at once, it let go. Sydney and Lindsey were both crying. "please mom lets leave," They both said. I knew after what it had just done to Sydney that we could no longer stay in the house. Just minutes before, I was ready to stay and take the beatings and never tell anyone that it was still there; All because I didn't want to disrupt our lives again. I knew I had to now. I would not let it hurt my children. I told the girls that I knew it was still there after I walked in the house and sat down. I didn't want to upset the girls so I tried to ignore it. I told them that I was sorry that I didn't tell them. I said, "your dad should be here anytime so ill tell him what's going on and we can leave." I heard Jake's car coming up the hill. I hated telling him because I knew that he would be mad. When Jake walked in, the girls ran over to him and they were both crying. Jake looked at me and I told him that it was still in the house. Jake said, "What!" Then he said, "Come on Cindy!" We started arguing about us staying. I couldn't believe he wanted us to stay. I walked over to the screened in porch, that's when I smelled it. That horrible smell was right by me. I could only smell it for a minute as if to say ha ha, I'm still here. I walked into the kitchen where Jake was sitting. The girls were sitting on the couch in the TV room right by the kitchen. We heard a loud banging noise coming from the TV room. The girls came running out. They looked at me and Jake and said, "It got between us and banged on the wall." I said, "That's it Jake. Cant you see that it is not just hurting me but its hurting our daughters? You like this hell hole so much, you stay, we are leaving." Before we left, I turned to him and said, "I smelled it again on the porch awhile ago." Jake decided he was leaving also. We all walked out together. When we got to the bottom of the hill, Jake turned to go to his mom's house and I turned to go to mine.

    I dreaded knocking on her door and telling her that we had to stay there again. I love my mom with all of my heart and I know she loves me but I also know that when your use to living by yourself that you are set in your own ways. I knew the kids and I were getting on her nerves; Me staying up all night praying and scared of every little sound. I asked God to give us all the strength to make it through this terrible time. I couldn't believe after all this time of waiting to go back home, that I was on my way back to my mom's house. Why was this happening to us again? I felt tears running down my face as I pulled up mom's hill. I told the girls to be quiet as I knocked on the door. One look at me and mom asked, "Cindy, what's wrong?" I said, "Mom, its still there." She said, "Oh, no." I said, "Mom, I'm sorry but me and the girls have no where to stay." She said that we were welcome to stay with her. I sat down trying to think. I said, "Mom, I think I will call the priest and tell him what happened." She told me to go ahead and call him and maybe he would come back. I picked up her phone and called him. When he answered I said, "Father Anderson, its still there. Why? How can this be! I thought after you came in, it would be gone." He said, "I don't know why its still there." I asked him if he would come back up to the house and do something different because obviously the holy water didn't work. Just like Katlin's ex husband Jeff said, it was too powerful for holy water. I told the priest what it had done to Sydney and Lindsey. He made it clear that he was not going back in the house. Before we hung up he said, "Cindy, when you feel the evil around you say, "David son of God have mercy on me." I asked, "Who is David? I always thought that Jesus was the son of God." He then asked me, "What religion are you?" I replied, "Baptist." He asked, "then why did you contact me in the first place?" I said, "because no one from any other churches would help me. They said they weren't prayed up enough to go in the house." He said, "ok Cindy, then you say Jesus son of God have mercy on me." Before we hung up, Father Anderson said something at my house earlier that day that I wanted to get cleared up. I said, "Today before you left you told me to quit leaving my body. Well I have no control over it. I do not make myself do it. Well thanks for all your help Father Anderson." When I hung up the phone, I looked at mom and said, "Well it looks like I'm on my own." She said, "You mean he's not going to help you?" I said, "No mom, he said he wants no part of it anymore. He said that he did all that he could do." I knew better. He was afraid just like everyone else. I didn't blame him, he was only human.

 Everyone got ready for bed. As for me, it was just one more sleepless night. I sat there thinking how unfair this seemed. All those weeks, everything I had been through. The physiological evaluation, running to get the deeds for the house, and talking to the priest., All for nothing. It was all false hope that I was given. I thought about Carrie and what she had said, "Get the light around you and get what you need, leave that house and never look back. Let the movers get the rest. It lives there, its always been there." and what about the priest? She had said to let her know if the priest could help me. Not let me know when the priest helps me; If, was the keyword. Carrie knew the whole time that I would have to move because the evil thing wasn't going to leave. I felt the presence of someone else in the room. I began praying. I was asked by Carrie or the priest if I had panic attacks. I had answered, "Yes." Which ever one who had asked me had told me that was when the spirits were around me. I felt really scared and I said aloud, "Jesus son of God, have mercy on me." My heart skipped a few beats. I repeated it. After I prayed my heart stopped skipping beats. I opened the bible and began praying. This went on all night long.

In the morning when mom got up, I told her I was going to call a realtor that had sold me the house and put it back on the market. She agreed that it would be the best thing to do. I called the office but the realtor wasn't in yet so I said that I would call her back. Jake called not to long after I had called the office. I told him that I was trying to get a hold of the realtor so I could put the house back up for sale. Jake said, "no Cindy, don't do that. Ill tear the house down and we could rebuild. Ill get my uncle to help us." I said, "Jake, its coming from under the house. There are people buried under there." He said, "Well then we will rent the house out and build another house on the hill in back." I said, "Jake you don't understand, bodies are buried all over that hill. I can't live anywhere near that house or the hill. Can't you see Jake, I took my money and instead of buying the house I wanted, I bought what you-wanted, a piece of hell. The devil himself lives in that house and it always has. Your name is not on the house, mine is. So you can either stand by me and try to help me or you can just walk away. I will sell the house with or without you." Jake started yelling at me. He said that he would burn the house down and dig the bodies up. I said, "Damn it Jake, it's smarter than you. Do you think it's really going to let you do that? It even tricked the priest!" I hung up on Jake. At that moment, I truly believed that I hated Jake. That house and all of that property meant more to him then I did. I began crying again.

When I calmed down enough, I called the real estate office again and spoke to the realtor who had sold me the house. I told her that I needed to put the house back up for sale. I explained a little bit about it over the phone as well as I could. I still couldn't speak very well. The realtor set up an appointment for me to come in to do the paper work. Jake called later to apologize to me. I told him I had an appointment with the realtor and he said he wanted to go with me. I felt better knowing he was going with me. I just wanted to put the house on the market and get it sold. Jake and I went together an explained what was happening in the house. Since there were two realtors that had sold us the house, they were both sitting there listening. I sat there wondering if they thought I was crazy. If that's what they were thinking, I didn't care, by this time, I felt like I was crazy. Maybe Jake was thinking the same thing because he said, "We have had a priest go into the house and before he would even go in, Cindy had to undergo a psychological evaluation test. She passed the test. She was told the only thing wrong with her was that she had too much psychic ability."

The realtors looked at me, and then looked at each other. They stepped out of the room for awhile. Jake and I sat in the room and waited for them to return. When they returned, they said that whoever was interested in buying the house, they would rather not mention anything that took place while I had lived there. Then remembered what Carrie had said, "as long as you are there, it will stay out." It was attracted to me. With someone else living there, it might not come out for another fifty years. I promised that I wouldn't say anything to anyone interested in buying the house.

Everything moved quickly after that. The House For Sale signs were put up. All I had to do now was wait for someone to buy it. When someone was interested in buying the house, the realtors would call moms and let me know. A week passed and I still hadn't got the call I had been waiting for. I had cried all that week. One day I was sitting there crying when Sydney and Lindsey came home from school. I heard Lindsey say, "She's crying again." Then I overheard her say, "She doesn't even look like mommy anymore." The girls ate supper and then played for awhile. I was sitting on the couch with the bible in my hands when I felt someone staring at me. I looked up and my eyes met Lindsey's. She said, "Mommy, you look old." I said, "Well thanks Lindsey that's just what I wanted to hear." Then I started yelling at her. "Lindsey, why don't you try not sleeping for months and see how great you look!" When I was getting up from the couch, I heard Sydney ask Lindsey why she had said that. Lindsey said, "Because its the truth." I walked into the bathroom and stood there looking in the mirror. I tried to avoid mirrors ever since I had seen that old lady but now I stood there staring at myself. I was always told that my eyes were my best feature. Even strangers had come up to me and told me that I had beautiful eyes. Now my eyes were all swollen and puffy, the sparkle was gone. I had lines around my eyes and face that hadn't been there before. My hair was dull and my shine was gone. This evil thing had changed everything about me, inside and out. I hated the frightened, weak, and ugly person I had become.

My mind went back to a few weeks ago; Jake had insisted that I be with him on New Years Eve. I told him no. I said that with me, Haley, and the girls staying at moms, there were just too many people. So he got this brain storm idea to rent a hotel room. He said, "Your moms not going anywhere, she always stays home on New Years Eve." He said, "please Cindy, we need to be alone." I told him that I would think about it and call him back. I talked it over with my mom and she agreed to watch the girls. So on New Years Eve when Jake came to pick me up, I told him I was taking the van and I would follow him. I saw him look down at my hands, I was holding the bible. Jake said, "Cindy, you of all people should know that they have bibles in the rooms." I said, "Well, I'm taking mine just in case." I got in my van and followed Jake. When we got to the hotel, Jake already had the key. We went up to the room. Jake turned on the TV. We were both laying on the bed watching TV when Jake started kissing me, I pushed him away. I said, "Stop it Jake." He asked me what was wrong. I replied, "I don't know Jake, you have been going up to the house feeding the dog so how do I know that the evil thing is not with you. You were doing a lot of strange things when we lived in the house. So how do I know that it is not in you? Jake, the truth is I'm afraid of you now." I jumped off the bed, got my purse and bible, and ran out the door. I heard Jake calling my name but I kept on going.

When I was on the highway, I noticed that Jake was in back of me and followed me to moms. I sat in the van; I was afraid to get out. Jake started yelling at me because I wouldn't open the door. I finally opened the door and got out. I said, "I'm going in the house, ill talk to you later." I turned and started to walk away. Jake grabbed a hold of my arm. He said, "Listen to me Cindy, I've been just as afraid of this evil thing as you are. I talked to someone at the church about it. Why do you think I hung the crucifix by the front door?" He said, "It's just me Jake. I love you and I want to be with you." He said, "please Cindy, I've already paid for the room, please come back." We both heard a car pulling up the hill. It was after midnight. When the car turned the corner, it was Haley. When she got out of the car, I said, "Haley what are you doing home so early?" she replied, "I was about to ask you the same thing." It turned out she just didn't feel like partying, which was very unusual for Haley. She asked me what we were going to do. Jake was looking at me waiting for an answer. I said that we were going to leave.

Jake and I went back to the hotel. When we got there, he asked if I was hungry. I said, "I guess so." We went to get something to eat. When we got back, we were laying on the bed and Jake asked, "Cindy, can I just hold you?" I replied, "Yes." I had the bible right next to me opened to Psalms 91. Jake said, "I don't know where Cindy is but I wish she would come back. I just want you back to normal. I want you to be yourself again." I said, "Jake, how do you think I feel? I can't even speak right. I'm afraid all the time, I never sleep." Jake said, "Cindy, just close your eyes and try to get some sleep." I said, I can't, I'm afraid of what might happen to me." We talked until daylight. I remember Jake falling asleep. I drifted off but it wasn't for long and I didn't leave my body. A few hours later, I said that I needed to get going so I could get back to moms and take care of the girls. Now standing in front of the mirror, I knew that what Jake had said was true,

Cindy was gone. I had no idea who this lifeless person was staring back at me. I got down on my hands and knees and prayed. I prayed for God to make me stronger and to be the person I use to be. When I came out of the bathroom, the phone rang. It was the realtor and told me someone wanted to look at the house. They would be there tomorrow afternoon. When I hung up the phone, I was happy. But then I thought about the snow and the mud. Jake had been feeding the dog so I knew the floors were tracked up with mud. I needed to go mop the floor. I called Jake and he told me that he would meet me in the morning after the girls were in school. I told mom since Jake would be with me, that I would take all the bed clothes and wash them at my house. She had a small apartment sized washer that had to be hooked up to the sink. So this would make it a lot easier on her.

The next morning after the girls were on the bus, I drove up to the house. I was glad to see Jake had already arrived. I told him that I had the bed clothes with me. He helped me carry them inside. At first I felt scared but then I started praying to myself. We put the clothes in the washer and I wiped up the floor. It wasn't as bad as I thought it would be. There was some mud but not a lot. Jake and I went into the TV room and sat down. Jake turned the TV on. We watched TV for awhile then I said, "Jake, I need to check the clothes." there was a divider that separated the TV room and the utility room. Jake had opened the divider when we first walked into the TV room. Since Jake could see me, I wasn't afraid. I was taking the clothes out of the washer and putting them into the dryer. I had my sleeves pushed up to my elbows. I went to turn the dryer on when all of the sudden I felt something wet on my arm. I said, "What the hell!" It was perfect droplets of water all up and down my arm. I looked up at the ceiling because I thought there was a leak, but there wasn't. I started walking very slowly towards Jake. I said, "Jake look!" The water droplets were still in place. He had a strange look on his face. I said, "The evil son of a bitch is throwing holy water back at me. Jake said "Cindy, there probably is a leak in the ceiling." I said, "No Jake, I checked." Jake said, "I have to go to the bathroom." On his way, I saw him stop and look up at the ceiling. Next I saw him touch it. He ran his hand all over. I saw him shake his head as if he couldn't believe it. When he came back in the room, I said, "I told you Jake, its throwing holy water back at me like the priest threw it on the walls." I guess it was trying to tell me that I wasted my time bringing the priests in the house, which I knew that already. It already showed me that when the girls and I came back that day. Maybe it was just trying to scare me. If that was the reason, then it had succeeded once again. I prayed for God to watch over us. I kept praying to myself. I could sense that something was around me. I didn't smell that bad smell but instead, I felt something as cold as ice right next to me. I told Jake that if the clothes didn't get dry soon, that I was going to take them back to moms damp. Mom had a little dryer and it would take forever for the bed clothes to dry. After I thought about it, I decided to wait. There was no sense of running her electric bill up more than I had to. As it was, I was up all night with the lights and TV on. I knew mom wasn't too happy about that. When the clothes were finished, I didn't even bother folding them, I pushed them all into the baskets and left.

When I got back over to moms, I told her how the evil thing had thrown the holy water back at me. She said, "Well Cindy, maybe the people that are going to look at the house today will buy it." I sure hoped so because that's what I was counting on. I called the realtor that evening. She said that they didn't seem all that interested. A few days later I heard the same thing about other couples. The wash was piling up once again. Jake said he would meet me up at the house to do the wash. We were in the TV room waiting on the clothes to dry when we heard a knock at the door. We both went to answer it. It was the realtor, she was showing the house. She said that she was sorry; she didn't know we would be there and it was a last minute thing. I said that it was ok to just sell the place. When the realtor was taking the couple through the house I looked up at a lady. I didn't know her by name but I had seen her around town. A few more couples came through while we were there. They were all local people that had nice houses. I looked at Jake and said, "These people are not interested in buying this hell hole, they just want a tour of the haunted house." All these people were just curious about the evil. I was very upset. Didn't these people know that they were giving me false hope? But then when I calmed down, I thought about the whole situation. I put myself in their place and I asked myself, wouldn't I be curious too? I spoke to the realtor about this. I said, "The whole town knows what has been taking place in this house, so anyone from Caseyville that's coming up to look at the house, is only doing it out of curiosity. She told me just to hang in there because people would be getting their income tax back soon. She said the advertisement for the house was in different counties. I said that I would have to hang in there because there was nothing I could do.

That evening back at moms, the girls were getting ready to take a bath and there was no shampoo. I had forgotten we were out. I told mom I was going to run to the house to get some. Sydney and Lindsey were getting on my moms nerves really bad so I told them to come with me. When we pulled up, Lindsey was reluctant about going in. She said, "I don't want to go in mommy." I said, "ok Lindsey, just stand on the porch." Since there was shampoo in both bathrooms, I wasn't about to go to the bathroom upstairs. I said, "I'm just going to the bathroom downstairs, I will be right back." I had just grabbed the shampoo when I heard Lindsey screaming at the top of her lungs. She yelled, "Help me! Help me! It's going to kill me!" I dropped the shampoo and ran to the porch where Sydney was yelling at Lindsey. I asked her why she was screaming like that. There wasn't anything wrong. I spoke up and said, "Lindsey, you almost gave me a heart attack." She said, "I told you that I didn't want to come with you. I hate this house!" I said, "Lindsey, get in the van and wait for me." I was still shaking from Lindsey's little ordeal. I went back in and I picked up the shampoo I had dropped. I locked up the house and drove off. I told myself that I didn't care how much Lindsey was getting on my mom's nerves that I would never make her go back in that house again. I told mom the same thing when I got back to her house.

Not long after that happened, mom was cooking something one evening and she discovered that she didn't have enough cooking oil. Instead of going to the store and buying some more, I offered to go to the house because I had a large bottle up there. I told mom that I would be right back when Lindsey said, "I'm not going with you." I said, "don't worry Lindsey, I wouldn't think of taking you again." I was sitting there wishing I wouldn't have opened my mouth because it was already dark out and I didn't want to go in by myself. I felt Sydney staring at me; it was as if she had read my mind. She said, I'll go with you mommy so you don't have to go by yourself." I asked, "are you sure Sydney?" She said, "yes mommy." Mom gave me a flash light so I could see to put the key in the lock. On our way up to the house; I started praying. When we pulled up the hill, the house looked scary. I shut the van off and took the flashlight and turned it on. As soon as I got in the house, I turned the lights on. I stood there asking myself, "Which cabinet had I put the oil in?" I looked in one cabinet and it wasn't there. I finally found it. I figured since I was already here that I should take some can goods back to moms with us. They weren't doing us any good sitting up there. I went over to the cafe doors and turned the light on. I went and grabbed a bag for the can goods in the utility room. I sat down on the kitchen floor and started taking the can goods out. I felt someone In back of me and I assumed it was Sydney. I was putting the can goods in the bag when I heard Sydney screaming, she hadn't been in the kitchen with me. The screaming was coming from the utility room. I jumped up and Sydney came flying through the cafe doors. Her face was beet red and she was shaking. She could hardly speak, she kept repeating, "Faces, faces, ugly faces mommy." She said, "please mommy, I want to leave." I went over to the utility room to turn the light off. I didn't see anything but I knew it was still there, it just wasn't appearing in front of me. I knew that if that would have happened to me, that I would be scared too. I'm not saying that I wasn't afraid because I was. When I walked into the room and looked around, I was more mad than scared. I said, "leave Sydney alone, stay away from her!" I turned the light out and I went back to the kitchen, grabbed our bag and went out the door. The house was once dark again as we drove away. I scolded Sydney. "What the hell were you doing in the utility room?" Sydney said, "I'm sorry mommy, I wanted to see my toys when faces came out of the wall at me. They were so ugly, I was so scared." I said, "I know you were and I'm sorry for yelling at you I know you miss your toys." I felt sorry for Sydney and Lindsey; they had been through so much. When we got back to moms, I told her what had happened. I said, "I just wish the house would sell and this nightmare would be over with."

More days had passed and still the house hadn't sold. One day while the girls were at school, I needed something from the house. I couldn't get a hold of Jake so mom said she would go with me. We weren't in the house very long when mom started getting sick. By the time we got back to her house, she was deathly sick. She was fine before we went up to the house. It made me stop and think. She had been up to the house twice with me and both times she got sick. I feared that somehow the evil was making my mom ill. My Fears were confirmed when I spoke to Carrie. I can't even remember what I had asked Carrie this time but she asked about mom. I told her how she got really sick. She said, "Cindy, don't let your mom go back in that house. As a matter of fact, keep her away from the hill; if you were smart, you would stay away also." She said one more thing before we hung up. She asked me if I knew that evil could go into anybody that I brought up there with me and that the person could hurt me without even knowing it. I once again thanked her for talking to me.

One evening Taylor and Tyler came over to Moms to visit. By then, I was a real basket case. I was holding the bible when they walked in. I noticed every time I looked at Tyler, he was staring at me, and then he would turn his head the other way. I guess he also wondered where his Aunt Cindy went. After all, I couldn't speak right and I was more like a robot than a human being, after they left to go home, I thought about Tyler and how close we use to be and it broke my heart because I could tell that he was scared. Later the phone rang and it was Taylor. She said, "Well when we left moms tonight, we were on our way home and Tyler said he was scared because he thought the evil thing was going to follow us home. I saw a church so we stopped. I told him that we could go in and speak to a priest then we could both feel better. As soon as we got out of the car, we started walking up the sidewalk towards the church. The church bells started going crazy. We kept walking and when we got to the front door of the church, it wouldn't open. I kept pulling on the door but it was locked. I told Tyler that something wasn't right. Someone should be there. Just then, a man came around from the back of the church. I asked him where the priest was and he said that he didn't know, that he was trying to find him too and he didn't know why the church bells were ringing like that. This is some weird stuff" Taylor Added. I said, "Taylor, go and get your bible. She said, "Cindy, its right here, I got it out as soon as we got in the house." I said, "Good, now open it to Psalms 91." She said, "your not going to believe this but when I opened the bible, that's where it was." I told her to get Tyler and read aloud 1-16. I told her to tell Tyler after she read it that they would be ok; that God would protect them. When we hung up, I wondered how many more of my loved ones this evil thing would try to destroy. I spoke to Taylor the next morning and she said that Tyler was up most of the night. She told me that he was still really scared and that she didn't think she was coming back up to moms for awhile. I told her that I understood.

One evening Kendra called and said, "What the hell did you stir up on this hill?" I asked her what was going on. She said, "You wouldn't believe the stuff that is going on in my trailer. We were so afraid last night that we called my aunt." She told me to get my bible and read Psalms 91. I don't know what the hell you stirred up on this hill; it was peaceful until you moved up here. I'm so scared now that I'm ready to move." I said, "I'm sorry Kendra." She said, "I know its not your fault, I just want you to know that its not just in your house but its in my trailer now." Not too long after that, Kendra called again. She and a cousin of hers had gone out one night; When they were coming home, she pulled up the driveway. She said her headlights hit the kitchen window of my house and they both saw a man standing in the window. She said, "your house was still dark but you could still see the silhouette of the man." They were afraid to get out of the car. Another person who had witnessed seeing the man in the window was my cousin Shellie, my uncle Todd's daughter. She liked to jog for exercise. She was on the back roads jogging when she went by my house and noticed something in the window. She stopped to get a closer look and she said that a man was in the upstairs window.

I went to check the mail one day; the mail box was at the bottom of the hill. I received a letter from my insurance man. I had my car and house insurance with the same company. In the letter, Dave, my insurance guy said that he had tried several times to reach me by phone but he couldn't get me. The letter asked me to please call the office that it had to do with dropping the car insurance from the car I signed over to Jake. When I got to moms, I called Dave. Dave had been up to take pictures of the house when he first insured it. I didn't say anything about my situation at first. Before we hung up he asked, Cindy, how do you like your new house?" I explained that the house was haunted and that I had been staying at moms for two weeks. He said, "your kidding." I made a big mistake by telling Dave that I wasn't living there because the very next day, I got a call saying that they were dropping the insurance on my house. I wasn't home when the call came but mom was. When I walked inside, she told me. I said, "oh no! God what am I going to do now?" I had several people offer to destroy the house but I had said no. now what if someone took it upon themselves to go ahead and destroy it? I would be stuck with a piece of hell the rest of my life. I called Dave and he said that he was sorry and that he was telling his boss about the house and he was afraid that someone would burn it down. I said, "Dave, the evil thing is not going to let anyone burn it down because it knows that it would burn with it but now that I'm not insured, other things could happen. Please Dave, tell your boss that I will move back in the house." We hung up and Dave promised to call me back." He did call me back. He said that his boss said whether or not I moved back, he wasn't going to insure it and he wanted no more to do with it. When I hung up, I started crying. I called the real estate office and spoke to the realtor. She said that the house can't even be on the market without insurance. I said, "Well, I'm out of money. I've been paying my mom so much on her bills plus the mortgage on the house plus all the bills at my house. I was laid off after Christmas so I have hardly anything left anymore. "She said, Cindy, I'll talk to the other realtor and see if we can help you. When we figure something out I will call you back.

If that wasn't bad enough, mom's landlord came and had a talk with her. The woman upstairs said my kids were making too much noise. When mom told me that I said, "You know better, that lady hates Haley, they never got along. Well I'll go upstairs and talk to her myself." Mom said, "No, you stay here, you're not going up there as mad as you are right now. You are going to end up getting me kicked out of here." I said, "Mom, you have been here for 13 years and she has lived her for about a year and you think you will get kicked out?" Mom smarted back off to me and she went into the other room. I sat there thinking about the situation, I knew I couldn't stay there any longer. Haley wasn't making it any easier. I had told her a while back that this was too much on mom and that she should stay at her own house. Haley always agreed but every night she was knocking on the door at 2 a.m. Haley had some guy living with her that was pretty wild otherwise I would be staying at her place. The longer I sat there, the more upset I got. "I will just go back up to the house," I said. My mom said, "No Cindy, I don't want you staying up there. When you calm down, just go up there and talk to her about the noise." When I went upstairs, I knocked on the door. At first there was no answer. I knew that they were home because I could see their car parked in the driveway and I also heard them walking around. If anyone should complain it should have been mom, you could hear that baby crying all the time. Finally her husband answered the door. I told him that I wanted to speak to his wife. She came to the door holding her baby. I asked, "Why did you tell the landlord that we were making too much noise?" she said, "Well I've been hearing your girls lately." I said, "Then why didn't you tell my mom like she asked you to do?" She didn't have an answer. I said, "Well you know what's been going on in that house. I'm trying to sell it and I don t appreciate you causing more trouble. So if you think we are making too much noise then you have my mom's number and you can call her and tell her, not the landlord." I went back downstairs. I couldn't take much more.

After that, mom quit talking to me and I quit talking to her. We started avoiding each other. You could feel the tension in the air. Haley even asked me what was going on. I told her that I guessed it was because we have been at moms too long and that it was too much on her. I called Jake and told him what was going on. He said that his dad was getting worse otherwise his mom would let us stay up there. When I hung up, I was really disappointed. After all, they had a large house with a basement. If it was up to Jake's dad, I know that he would have told us to come on over and stay. Well I guess I shouldn't have been mad, Jake's mom had lot on her. I sat there figuring out where we could go. I saw mom looking at me and I blew up. Lindsey started crying, "Mommy what's wrong with you?" I never screamed and yelled at my mom like that before and Lindsey was scared. Sydney was crying too. I kept screaming then I started crying. I said, "Mom we are leaving and I don't know where were going but were leaving." I grabbed a few things and I told my girls to come on. Lindsey stood by mom. She was still crying when she said, "Your crazy, I'm not going with you." I said, "Suit yourself." I noticed that mom was crying which was something in all my years had not seen her do much. I went out the door and Sydney followed me. Sydney and I drove around half the night. Sydney was tired and I was getting tired of driving. Thank God I had some money. I pulled into a cheap motel. I asked to see a room. When the lady unlocked the door she turned on the light switch and I saw roaches everywhere. They were running up and down the walls. I looked over at Sydney, she looked so tired. But as tired as she was, I wasn't about to stay in this roach infested motel. I looked at the lady and told her that I changed my mind. I didn't need a room after all. When Sydney and I got back into the van, she asked, "Where are we going mom?" I answered her truthfully, "I don't know Sydney but if you have to sleep in the car all night it would be better than having bugs crawling on you." I knew that mom would let us come back, she never told us to leave in the first place. I felt terrible about the way I had screamed at her. It wasn't her fault that everything was so screwed up. Lindsey was right, maybe the evil thing had pushed me over the edge and I was crazy now. I started crying. I thought about everything. I knew I had hurt my mom deeply and that's what bothered me more than anything. My mom and I had always been so close, we were more like best friends than mother and daughter and now that evil thing destroyed even that. I drove around a little more. We had a house yet we were homeless.

I finally drove back to moms. When I pulled in the parking lot, I noticed Haley and Uncle Randy were there. I just sat there thinking about what a mess everything had become. I looked over at Sydney and she had fallen asleep. I said, "God please help me." When I was younger, my mom had told me, "Cindy, God never puts more on a person than he thinks the person can take." I said to myself, "So what happened God? I don't understand. I feel as if I'm carrying the weight of the whole world on my shoulders. I can't do it anymore. As of now, I'm putting my life and my daughters life in your hands. So God please help us because I don't know what to do anymore." Haley came outside and asked, "What did you say to grandma?" I said that I didn't even know what all I said. The only thing I did know was that I was sorry. I told Haley that everything just got to me. She told me that the guy that stays at her house wasn't going home tonight so we could stay at her house. I needed to apologize to mom but I was too ashamed to face her right then. I told Haley to go get Lindsey and see if she wanted to stay at her house, that way mom could be by herself for awhile. I told Haley that I would meet her at her house. If you went the short way to Haley's house, you would have to go past my house, so I took the long way. When we got to Haleys, she was already there. We talked for awhile and then got the kids ready for bed.

It was really late when we heard a knock at the door. It was Haley's cousin Kara. I bet we looked like a sight, the girls and I were laying in the living room and me with the bible in my hands opened up to Psalms 91. Haley took Kara in the other room and explained what was going on. Kara had asked Haley when she found out that I had bought the house, wondered why i would even want "The Amityville Horror House" for. Everyone said that it looked like that house and it really did. We stayed at Haleys for a few days when my uncle Randy got a hold of me. He said that mom was really worried about me and that I should call her. He said that mom was really depressed. I said, "I thought she would be glad that we were gone. I know I would after the mess we made out of her life." I did call her and apologize to her. She wanted me to come up and talk to her. I told her I would come up after the girls were out of school. We were both crying when we hung up. Haley said the guy that was living with her was moving out and if we wanted to keep staying with her that we could. She didn't want to stay by herself anyway.

The rent was due soon so I gave her some money to put towards the rent. When it was time for the girls to get to school, I went and picked them up. I told them that I had spoken to grandma and she wanted us to go to her house. When we got there, we talked for a long time and we both agreed that we were under a lot of stress. She said that she wished that we would come back to her house and stay. I said that maybe we could stay at her house sometimes and some at Haley's house. That way we wouldn't be getting on each others nerves.

One night when I was staying at Haley's house, I was really tired and the girls were already asleep. I was reading Psalms 91 when I felt as if I couldn't keep my eyes open any longer. Then it happened, I was out of my body. I don't know where I was but I didn't get hit. When I was back in my body I sat up and looked around. I had that feeling like someone was around me again. I noticed that Haley had left the kitchen light on and it started flickering. I began praying once again. The next day, I was over at moms when the realtor called and said that someone from out of town wanted to look at the house. She told me she would be showing it at the end of the week. So I had two days to get up there and dust the furniture, mop the floor, and to make it look like someone was living in it. I decided to stay at moms that night. I told the girls to keep their fingers crossed that whoever looked at the house would buy it. The next morning, I was surprised when Sydney said, "Mom, if you want to go clean the house I will go with you." I asked her if she was sure that she wanted to go up there and she said yes. It was strange, when I was in the house with Sydney, I wasn't as afraid. Maybe it was because I didn't want anything to hurt Sydney. When she was around, I felt like I had the strength to fight back. We got ready to go. When we pulled up the hill, I wasn't as afraid as I use to be. We walked in and I said, "What a mess!" The floor was full of mud and the downstairs furniture was full of dust. I said, "Well Sydney, I think I'll start with the floor." I had given Sydney some change to play with and she was sitting at the kitchen table playing with it. I got a bucket of soapy water and a rag. I put my hand in the water but it was way too hot. I stood there for a minute looking at Sydney; she had a lot of guts coming after what happened to her the last time she was here. I was so proud of her. I took the rag out of the bucket and I began squeezing the water out of it. I got down on my knees and began wiping the mud up. I felt something around me. I looked at Sydney and she was fine. I began praying to myself. All of the sudden I was pushed so hard that it knocked the breath out of me for a minute; I landed on the floor. Sydney screamed, "Mommy, are you ok?" I turned around and said, "I'm fine Sydney." I started saying, "Jesus son God have mercy on me." I said it over and over. I also kept saying that God was stronger than evil. I was almost done with the floor when Sydney said, "Mommy, its taking my money." I watched as the money went flying across the table. Sydney had been counting it when it started taking it from her. I said, "its ok Sydney, God is stronger than evil." I told her to say that out loud and she did. I tried to hurry through with what was left to do. I asked Sydney if she was scared, and she said no. We went into the TV room so I could hurry up and dust. While we were in there, I turned on the TV as if nothing had happened. When I was through, I turned off the TV and we began walking out of the room. The TV came back on so I turned around and turned it back off. I started to walk away when it came back on again. Now I was mad. I said, "Do you want to play games? Well then you can go to hell!" I unplugged the TV and Sydney and I walked out the door. That day was the best day I had in a long time. I'm not going to say that I wasn't scared at all but I wasn't half as scared as I use to be and that was a start.

Day by day I would get a little bit stronger. I can't remember now if the people came to look at the house didn't show up or they just weren't interested in the house. I was tired of dragging clothes and bed clothes back and fourth from moms to Haleys. I also started staying at moms more than I did at Haleys. She had so many people coming in and out of there at all hours of the night. I would meet Jake up at the house at least once a week to do the wash. I was ok in the house as long as I had someone with me. I always felt cold air around me. One morning, me and Jake were sitting on the couch waiting for the clothes to finish when I said, "Jake I'm freezing." He gave me a funny look and said, "Cindy, you're closest to the front door, that's why you are so cold." I asked him if he was cold and he said, "No, not really." I said, "Jake I don't think that the cold air is coming from outside. Besides I feel like someone's watching us." I knew the feeling I had all too well. I began praying to myself. Jake said, "Cindy, you're just cold blooded." I answered, "Yeah right!" A few times when I was in the house with Jake, I would get stuck or burned.

One day Allie called me and said her mom had told her aunt about my house. Her aunt had a neighbor named Rick Smith. He was a student at Washington University. He was very interested in the house because he was studying haunted houses. He wanted to know if I would let him and some of his classmates come up to the house. I said, "Allie, I don't know.

What if something would happen to them?" She said, "Well, it's up to you Cindy." I told her to let me think about it. I called back and got Ricks phone number. I called Rick and I told him that I wasn't responsible if anything bad should happen to anyone. He assured me that I wouldn't be responsible. I gave him my mom's phone number and told him to call me back with a day and a time he wanted to go up there. Before I hung up, I asked him if he believed in God and he said, "Yes." I told him that I didn't want anyone in the house that didn't believe in God. Rick called me back and told me what day he wanted to meet me at the house. I told him I was really nervous about taking him and his classmates to the house. When I told Jake about the people from the university, he blew up. He said, "Cindy, you have no business taking anyone up to that house." I tried to explain to Jake that they had been studying haunted houses and they knew a lot about them. Maybe they could help me in some way. We argued about it. It ended with me telling him that I had listened to him before and bought the house and look what happened. So whatever I did now would be none of his business.

The day came when we were to meet. I prayed for God to watch over us. I met the students at the house. They all seemed really nice. At first, I was really nervous but then after awhile I became more comfortable with them. They wanted to know which wall all of the spirits came out of. I took them upstairs and pointed at the wall. One of them said, "Feel the temperature from here to here." They started walking back and fourth. One student was standing in the middle of the room. I was sitting on the couch watching him when he jumped. He said that a blast of cold air had just gone around him. I said that I knew because after it went around him, it came around me. It had been traveling so fast that it made a whizzing noise around me. There was a female student standing in front of my girls' closet. She was pointing up and telling some of the other students that it looked like blood but it was running the opposite direction. I walked over and looked. It did look like dried blood. I had never noticed it before. They walked around checking all the rooms out. Someone started asking me questions, when I looked up; someone had a camcorder aimed at me. I didn't really like that. I didn't want to be recorded. They went around to each room recording. When they were through, we got ready to leave. It wasn't so bad; at least nothing bad had happened. I looked at Rick and said, "Well what do you think?" He said, "There's a haunting going on here." I already knew that but I didn't say anything. I guess these students couldn't really help me; but maybe I had helped them in some way with their studies. I went back to moms and told her and the girls what had gone on.

The next day, Rick called and asked me if him and his friend could come up to the house. This time they would be bringing some equipment with them to detect when this thing was around I said that I would let them do it. There was only one thing that bothered me. Rick said that this time we would have to turn the lights off. In the two months that I had lived in that house, I had never sat in any room with the lights off, even when I was blowing light bulbs there were always other lights on. Now Rick was asking me if I was willing to sit on the couch upstairs in the dark. He said that he and his friend would make sure nothing would happen to me. When we had hung up, I wondered what I had just done. I remembered what Carrie had told me about how this evil thing could get into a human and attack someone without the person knowing it. The more I thought about it, the more frightened I became.

The evening I was to meet the students, I was really scared. I told Haley what I had committed myself to and how frightened I was now. Since Rick and his friend weren't meeting me until real late, Haley said that she would meet me at the house around midnight. She said she had a date but she would make sure that she was with me so I didn't have to be alone with the students; that made me feel better. Since the police already knew about the house, I decided to go by the police station and talk to one of the officers. I told the officer what was supposed to take place after midnight. I asked if he would please patrol the area because sometimes my phone didn't work and if something would happen, then I might not be able to get help. It was still daylight and the officer said, "Ill go up there with you right now to check your phone." We left the police station and he followed me to my house. When we got in the house, he picked up my phone and he got a dial tone. I said, "Well, that's good it's working now but that doesn't mean it will still be working hours from now." He said, "Don't worry; someone will be patrolling the area." We walked out of the house together. I drove down the hill and went back to moms to wait until it was time to go back to the house.

As the time grew nearer, I was ready to back out. Haley had left hours ago to go out. I just hoped that she would keep her word and show up for me. I knew Haley like I knew the back of my hand; So I was afraid that she would start partying and forget all about me. I had told her before she left to go out that if she didn't show up that I would never forgive her. When it was time to go, I began praying. I was driving up the hill hoping Haley was outside sitting in her car waiting for me. Haley wasn't there but Rick and his friend were. I parked the van. I got out and told the guys that my niece was suppose to meet me here. They said they hadn't seen anyone. They were anxious to get started. Rick had introduced his friend to me but I was worried about Haley and didn't pay much attention. When we entered the house, we went straight up the stairs. I remember thinking, "Damn it Haley, you know how scared I am. Where the hell are you?" I tired not to let the guys know I was scared. We were sitting upstairs when we heard a noise downstairs. We had been talking but now it was so quiet you could have heard a pin drop. We just sat there looking at one another. Then I heard a familiar voice, it was Haley. She was yelling something from the bottom of the stairs. Haley couldn't hide the fact that she had been drinking. I wondered what good she would be now if something should happen. Rick started explaining about the equipment he brought. He made it himself. There was a handle and at the end what looked like a speedometer. It had numbers and the hand moved when it had something moving around it. He said that his teacher was out of the country so he couldn't get the schools equipment without the teacher's approval. I told him that it was ok with me; I just wanted to get this over with. Rick checked the equipment and it was working fine. He asked if I was ready. I started to answer yes when Haley said, "Wait a minute! What if something happens to my aunt? I bet your asses would be the first ones down the stairs." I said, "Haley, knock it off right now!" I was so embarrassed by Haley's behavior. The guys tried to assure her they wouldn't leave no matter what happened. I was asked again if I was ready. I answered, "Yes." The lights had only been off for a minute when I said, "Turn the lights back on!" All eyes were on me when the lights came back on. They asked, "What's wrong?" I knew the evil thing was somewhere in the room, I could feel it. I wanted to get up off the couch and run down the stairs and just keep running, far away from this hell hole that was called a house. I didn't get up and run, instead I answered their question. I said, "I just got scared, I could feel it. It's in the room with us." Rick said, "Cindy, when it gets by you tell me." I said, "Ok." The lights were out once more and I sat in the dark waiting. I felt it and I said, "Its here now, it's by me! Turn the lights on!" The lights went on. I looked over at Rick and he had a strange look on his face. He was looking at the speedometer. He said, "It broke it, it broke the equipment! I can't believe it! The hands went all the way around." He said, "When my teacher gets back, I'll bring the school's equipment." We all walked out together. Rick said, "I'll be getting in touch with you." I said, "Ok." They said thanks for letting them come up. I told Haley to leave her car and ride with me; I would bring her back in the morning. I was driving down the hill when I put my foot on the brake and the pedal went all the way to the floor. I said, "Oh shit Haley, I don't have any brakes!" by the time I reached moms hill, my breaks were fine once again. When we got in moms house, Haley started talking, she asked, "Cindy, you know when the lights were out?" I answered, "Yes." She said, "I saw something weird." I asked, "What?" She said, "Your exercise bike, it looked like the handle bars were moving." I said, "You saw it too? Haley, I didn't say anything about it because I knew that it wasn't possible. You can't move the handle bars on that type of bike." Haley said, "I know Cindy, that was weird." I said, "Well Haley, I've seen stranger things in that house. Things that I would never dream possible. If I wouldn't have seen them with my own two eyes, I don't think I would have believed it." That night, I fell asleep but I didn't leave my body. Around that time, I started sleeping. I never slept like a normal person but I was getting four or five hours of sleep. That alone helped me look and feel better. As for Rick, I never heard from him again. I had put a lot of distance between Jake and myself. I just didn't have the same feelings for him anymore. I was still running back and forth from my moms to Haleys.

One morning after I stayed at Haley's house, I drove the girls to school then I headed for moms. I noticed a police car in back of me and when I turned to go up mom's hill, he followed me. When I parked the van and got out, the policeman asked me if I stayed at the house last night. I said, "no way!" He said, "I didn't think so." He told me after midnight, all the lights were on. I told him that it was the ghost. I also told him that he wasn't the first person to tell me about the lights.

Kendra called and told me that she hadn't seen Jake lately. That meant that he wasn't feeding the dog. It was a beautiful day and I longed to be outside. I sat there for awhile and then I decided I would go up and feed the dog myself. It was still wintertime but the sun was out and I felt really good as I drove up the hill. When I parked the van, I got out and walked over to the dog; She was happy to see me. She jumped up and started licking me. Since I really didn't want to go in the house by myself, I unleashed her and said, "Come in." She followed me to the porch and I unlocked the door. I coaxed her into the house but she wouldn't go any further than the door. I left the door wide open. In case something would happen, I could run straight out the door. The dog was sitting against the door facing the upstairs. I was turned around at the kitchen sink filling her bucket with water. All of the sudden, I heard the dog making a strange growling noise. I turned around and she was between the bottom steps and the door. She was barking real loud when I noticed I could see her breath; she was looking at something by the stairs. I stood there for a moment thinking, "It's warm in here, why can I see her breath?" I sucked my own breath in and blew it out. I went all around the kitchen but I couldn't see my breath. Then all at once, I knew what was going on. I remember thinking, "Oh God it's by the dog, I have to get out of here!" I began praying as I took her food and water and walked by the dog. The dog followed me outside. I stood there for a few minutes before locking and slamming the door shut. Then I got the dog back where she belonged. I was shaking so bad I could hardly get her leash back on. I was still shaking when I drove down the hill. I decided I would never again go in the house alone.

    I received a call from the realtor; She sounded excited. She said she had shown the house to someone that was really interested. She said, "Cindy, she is from out of town and she is making an appointment to bring her boyfriend back to look at the house." Although it sounded real good, I hated to get my hopes up too high. I had already been let down enough. All I could do was hope and pray that this was the person who was sent to answer my prayers. While I waited for the realtor to let me know something, I stayed at moms.

    I was sitting talking to mom one evening when the phone rang. Mom had answered it and talked for a few minutes then handed me the phone saying it was Bridget. I hadn't spoken to Bridget in a long time. We had met when I was seventeen years old. She was around ten years older than me but when we first met, we instantly became good friends. I think it had been around a year since I had spoken to her; At least it seemed that long. It was good hearing her voice. She was telling me that someone had told her about the trouble I was having in the house. The person that told her didn't believe it because they knew the previous owners. Bridget told this person if I said that it had happened then it happened. She knew me well enough to know I didn't go around lying. Bridget wanted me and the girls to come over. She wanted to know all about the house. I said, "Sure, we can get out of mom's hair for awhile." I told her that we had been staying at moms and Haleys. When I hung up, I told mom that we were going to Bridget's for awhile. When we got to Bridget's, I began telling her about the house. By now, I could speak again. I don't even remember when I started speaking normal again. I had told Bridget how I couldn't speak right for months. Sometimes I studdered when I spoke about the house but nothing like before. Bridget said she wanted to go up to the house just to see if the evil thing would do something. I said, "I don't know Bridget, What if something happens?" I told her about it breaking Rick's equipment. She didn't seem to mind. She said she had read a lot of books on haunted houses but had never been in one. She said she had met the previous owners and had been up to the house before with a friend but everything seemed normal then. I finally told Bridget I would take her to the house.

    The first time I took Bridget to the house, nothing really happened; Nothing that she could see anyway. I remember getting stuck and burned.

We stayed downstairs and sat at the kitchen table. I felt cold air around me but nothing happened to Bridget. After that, Bridget called me again wanting to spend the night at the house. I said, "I don't know, I haven't spent the night there since that evil thing had went into Lindsey and spoke to me." Bridget wouldn't take no for an answer so I finally said that I would only if she promised not to go to sleep. I told her if I went to sleep and left my body that I would get beat really bad. Her husband Doug was against it from the start. He said he didn't believe in any of it. Why we set it up on a school night, I don't know but we did. Mom didn't seem overjoyed with the fact that I was spending the night in the house. Sydney said that if I were staying, then she was staying too. I said, "I don't know Sydney." I called.Kendra and told her what we were doing. She said that Brett could play with the girls. I said, "Well Lindsey said she won't go." I told Kendra, mom wasn't very happy with me and I didn't want to leave Lindsey with mom. She was stuck with her most of the time. When Lindsey didn't want to stay at Haley's house she would have to stay at moms. Kendra said, "I'm going out tonight but tell Lindsey that Brett can spend the night in the house with the girls." That did the trick. She said, "If Brett could stay, then she would." When it was time to meet Bridget, we left moms house and headed over to what everyone now called, "The Spook House." Brett was waiting for us. He was happy to be able to stay with the girls. When Bridget arrived, she had her daughter Tara with her. Tara was still in school, I think she was in 10th grade at the time. We sat around at the kitchen table talking. We had been there for hours and nothing happened. The kids were in the TV room watching television; it started getting really late. The kids had fallen asleep. We were talking and I said, "Listen." There was a religious program on TV and I could hear the preacher preaching something about God. I Said, "Something will happen now because the evil doesn't like anything to do with religion." About that time, we decided to go to the bathroom. When one of us had to go, we all walked in the utility room together and waited for our turn. When everyone was through, we would walk back into the kitchen. We all took our turns and when we were ready to go back into the kitchen, Tara stopped and looked at herself in the mirror. All of the sudden, a loud hissing noise came out of the wall at us, we started screaming and all three of us were trying to get out of the café doors at once. When we finally got through the doors, we all started running for the door that led outside. No one was thinking when Bridget yelled, "Stop! What the hell are we doing?" then Bridget said, "Listen." Tara and I looked at one another, we didn't hear anything. Bridget said, "The TV is off." We looked around the corner at the kids. They were sound asleep and the TV was off. "I said, "I told you the evil thing doesn't like religion."

Bridget said, "Do you realize that we were going to leave these children in this house by themselves." Where were we going? Nobody even had car keys on them. We all needed to calm down, Tara said, "I want to go home." Bridget asked Tara, "Why the hell did you have to look in that mirror to begin with." Tara said, "Please mom, just take me home." Bridget said, "No, you wanted to stay here so you're staying." We were all sitting at the table talking when we heard someone kick the door. Not the outside door but the door in the kitchen on the inside where we were sitting. Tara held a crucifix against her. We had brought flashlights just in case the lights went out but I was hoping that they wouldn't. It would be daylight in a few hours then we could get out of this place. I looked over at Tara, she was so afraid. She was lying on the kitchen floor crying holding a crucifix on her chest. I was thinking maybe I shouldn't be bringing people up to the house. Finally daylight came; I knew we were all relieved to be going. Bridget told Tara that even though she didn't get much sleep, she still had to go to school. I got the kids up and sent Brett home. We started straightening up what mess we made. When we got done, it was time to go. We all walked out together. I fed and watered the dog before we left. Bridget told me to call her later. I took the girls back to mom's house and got them ready for school. I was just sitting around when I decided to call Carrie. She told me if I spoke with Kurt the man who gave my sister Carrie's number. Maybe he could help me understand things better. She said that he had an occult shop in St. Louis, MO. She gave me his phone number.

When we hung up, Bridget called me and invited me and the girls to stay at her house. I told her what Carrie had said about Kurt. Bridget said that Doug had an appointment at Barnes hospital the following week. She said, " Cindy, get the address of the occult shop and see if you can meet him on that day." when Bridget and I hung up, I called Kurt's occult shop. We spoke on the phone a few minutes and then he gave me his address and said that he would be happy to meet me. I told him I would be getting a ride from a friend and about Doug's doctors appointment. We set a time that we would meet at his shop. I called Bridget and told her what Kurt had said. She was as anxious as I was to see what he had to say about everything that was going on. The girls and I ended up spending the whole weekend at Doug and Bridget's house. On Sunday morning, I thanked them for letting us stay with them then we headed back to mom's house. When I got to moms, she said that Jake was upset because he hadn't spoken to me in awhile. Mom said she told him that we were staying at Bridget's and Doug's.

A few days later, I was on my way to St. Louis with Doug and Bridget. We went to Barnes hospital first. It didn't take long at all at the hospital.

What did take long was the ride to the shop; it was way out in Missouri. When we arrived, there was a lady behind the counter. I explained that I was supposed to meet Kurt. She said for me to stay put that Kurt had just called and said he was running late. She said that he also told her to tell me that he will be there as soon as possible. I had never been in an occult shop before and I really didn't know what to expect. Doug, Bridget and I started walking around the shop looking at everything. The more I looked, the more scared I became. I wondered what kind of man Kurt was. There were black candles as well as white. He had oils, incense, and all kinds of herbs. He had books on magic, esp., astrology, you name it and he had it. I guess it was the voodoo dolls that scared me the most. I looked at Bridget and said, "This place gives me the creeps." I said, "Bridget, I want to leave." She said, "No Cindy, just wait and talk to the man." I said, "Bridget, a lot of this stuff represents evil to me." she said, "Well, still stay and see what he has to say." Kurt walked in right after Bridget told me to stay. I introduced myself and Doug and Bridget. He started talking to me and he said, "Cindy your doing this yourself." I yelled, "What!" I was so mad. I said, "I am not hitting myself! I have been beaten so bad that I thought I was going to die." What was he doing? Trying to make me look like a nut case? I felt the tears in the corners of my eyes. I stood there thinking, "Don't cry." I bit my lip and stood there staring Kurt right in the eyes. He said, "your making this happen yourself." I looked at Bridget; she was looking at me then at Kurt. Kurt then asked, "did you want to buy the house?" I answered truthfully, "No, I didn't. I wanted a different house but my boyfriend Jake talked me into buying it." Then Kurt asked, "Are you happy with the man that lives with you?" Again I answered, "No." Kurt said, "you have poltergeist under your house and spirits in your house. By you being so unhappy, you brought the evil out. I suggest you sell the house and get away from your boyfriend." I couldn't see where Kurt had been such a big help to me.

On the way home, Doug stopped so we could get something to eat. I didn't feel like eating though. I was glad to be back in Illinois. I felt really drained. When I got back to Doug and Bridget's, I used their phone to call Carrie and tell her what Kurt had said. Carrie said, "Yes, there are poltergeist under your house and there are spirits in your house but your own psychic ability brought it out not your unhappiness." I said, "That's what really threw me off when he had said that." I was thinking that I wasn't that unhappy when I was moving in. Jake and I had even discussed knocking the wall out in the TV room to make it larger. I had high hopes for that house. True, it wasn't the house that I wanted but I was going to make the best out of it to keep the peace. Before we hung up, Carrie said, "Why are you bringing people into that house?" I answered her curiosity. I said, "The people are curious about the house and asked me to take them in to see if they could see anything." Carrie said rather sharply, "Cindy, don't take anyone else in that house because someone is going to get hurt." I said that I wouldn't and I hung up the phone. I repeated what Carrie had said to Bridget. I told Bridget that we weren't going to go up there anymore. She agreed and we stayed away from the house. Jake called moms when I got home. He said he spoke to his mom and she said I could spend the night with him at her house Saturday night. I asked, "What about the girls?" He said, "Dads not doing too good, can't your mom or Haley take the girls?"

That Saturday, mom took Lindsey and Haley, took Sydney. I stayed with Jake and when it was time to go to bed I said, "Jake I need a bible." He said, "it's late and everyone is asleep upstairs and we are down in the basement." I said, "Jake, I will not sleep without a bible and mine is at moms." He said, "You will be ok Cindy, I wont let anything hurt you." I said, "Like before Jake? I'm leaving; I'm going back to my moms." He said, "No wait, ill go find one." I really didn't feel safe there to begin with; our hills were too close together. I heard Jake telling his mom that I wouldn't go to sleep without a bible. A few minutes later, Jake came downstairs with a bible. When Jake finally fell asleep, I laid there listening to him sleep. I thought back to when I was younger, There was a place called Cannon Ball Hill. My grandmother and grandfather lived close by the hill. I couldn't have been more than nine years old when I was visiting my grandparents and my uncle nick asked me to go to Cannon Ball Hill with him. I told him that I wanted to go. I was excited, I heard Nick and his brother Todd talk about the hill but I had never been there. When we got there, I had the weirdest feeling that I had been there before. I stood on the hill looking around. I knew we were the only ones on the hill but I felt like someone was watching us. In a way, it was kind of scary because there were only woods around us. A few years later, I was in 5th grade and the place to hang out was at Cannon Ball Hill. There was an old milk truck that everybody played in. I remember the first time I went to Cannon Ball Hill with my friends; I had the same weird feeling that I had when Nick first brought me on the hill. I was standing there thinking about it when one of my friends interrupted my thoughts. She was asking me if I had heard her. I said, "I'm sorry, what did you say?" She asked me what I was thinking about. I said, "I was here a few years ago with Nick and I had the strangest feeling that I had been here before. I have the same feeling now." I didn't tell her that I had a feeling that someone was watching us. When I got home, I told my mom of my feelings. She said, "Cindy that's called Dejavu. She explained Dejavu to me. Well I guess that's what it was, my feelings of being there before but that didn't explain the presence that I had felt. Now sitting there watching Jake snore. I remembered him being on Cannon Ball Hill with the rest of us. Cannon Ball Hill was very close to my hill and even Jake's mom's hill were all fairly close together. I wondered if they all had bodies buried somewhere. I never did go to sleep that night. Then daylight came, I was sitting up. Jake asked, "What are you doing up so early?" I told him that I had never went to sleep.

The realtor called moms to let me know that the women that had looked at the house wanted to buy it., her boyfriend liked it. Finally, I would get rid of the house once and for all. The realtor said that they were going to see if they could get a loan to buy the house and she would get back to me as soon as she found out something. Nick called my moms and said, "I need to ask you something and I wont get mad if you say no." I said, alright." He said, "Debra's sister and some people she works with wanted to take a tour of your house." Nick and Debra had done a lot for me so there was no way I was going to turn them down. I said, "Just let me know what night you want to do it and give me a time." He asked, "Are you sure you don't mind?" I said, "No, I don't care but it has to be soon though because I might have the house sold." He called back to tell me he wanted to come the following week, I said that it was fine with me.

I spoke to Bridget and told her about Nick calling me, she said that she wanted to go up to the house too. Jake called me, I told him what was going on. He said, "are you crazy? You're not taking people up to that house!" I said, "Watch me." I spoke to Bridget later and I ended up at her house. The next day Jake was really mad because he drove by Bridget's and saw my van. I had been spending a lot of time at Bridget's since she first called me and Jake hated that. The day arrived when we were to meet Nick at the house. When the time grew nearer, Sydney decided that she was going with me. Lindsey said that she was never going back to the house again. Mom said that she would watch Lindsey. When it was time to go, we headed for the house. Me, Bridget, and Sydney were in the house when Jake and Doug showed up. Jake knew I was mad. I told him he better not start anything or do anything to embarrass me. When Bridget and Doug were talking, I asked Jake why he had come to the house. He said that he wanted to be with me. Sydney was the only one happy because she missed Jake. Nick knocked on the door, I told him to come in. Debra was in back of him and then a few women then a man and then I lost track. There were so many people. Nick walked over to me and said, "Cindy, I'm sorry, I didn't know she was bringing so many people until she met us to come over. I said, "Its ok." I just hoped that Jake would keep his mouth shut. Nick started taking everyone upstairs. Jake started mouthing off. When I walked over to Jake, I smelled the Alcohol. I wasn't too happy with him to begin with, now I was really mad. I said, "Jake, don't even come upstairs, stay in the TV room with Doug." Sydney said she wanted to stay downstairs with the men and watch TV. Bridget and I went upstairs. Everyone started asking questions. We were answering them when a few people said they wanted to have a tea reading. I said, "I don't think that's a good idea." Half of the people agreed with me and the other half were for it. One of the women walked into the kids' room and a few others followed and shut the door. One woman was really scared and said, "I'm going to see what's going on in there." She poked her head in the room and said, "Their having a tea reading." That was going too far. I didn't like what was going on here at all. Nick said, "I'm sorry Cindy." I said, "Its really not your fault Nick." When they were through, they came out of the room. One lady went back in the room and turned out the light then the door shut. I said, "What is she doing in there?" It started getting real hot in the room. We were all sitting in the upstairs living room. I couldn't understand it, usually when this thing came out it would get real cold. Everyone was complaining about how hot it was getting. I heard the lady scream the name Steven. She said it a few times then you could hear her getting knocked into the wall. She was really screaming now. I looked at Bridget and asked, "What the hell is going on in there?" We were getting scared so me and Bridget headed for the stairs. Just then the door flew open and the lady came out. Her lip was all swollen and there was blood running out of it. She looked at us and said, "It's evil." she was crying. That was it, these people had to go. We walked downstairs and I said, "Damn, it's hot in here." Jake and Doug started laughing. I asked, "What is so funny?" Then I asked "What did you guys do?" I walked over to the thermostat and it was close to 100 degrees. Jake said, "Cindy, they wanted to feel hell, I just helped them along." I said, "Real cute Jake. I hope your still laughing when I give you the gas bill to pay this month." I was so mad at Jake. I told him to leave. Bridget asked me, "do you think this is what the psychic was talking about when she said someone was going to get hurt?" I said, "Oh, Bridget I forgot all about that. That's it! I'm not bringing anyone back in this house."

 The girls and I had been staying at moms for a week straight. I knew the girls were starting to get on moms nerves again. I wasn't much better. I was a nervous wreck wondering if the people from out of town had heard if their loan went through or not. It seemed to me that it was taking longer than necessary. I had spoke to Taylor on the phone and told her about the people wanting to buy the house. She asked me if the house sold if I was going to buy another house. I said, "I don't know. I've been thinking about that. I really don't want to pay rent but on the other hand, I can't afford a brand new house. Do you think if I would find a house, the owners would agree to let me spend the night in it for two weeks and see if there's poltergeist or spirits in it? I don't think so. I guess ill just get stuck renting again. I really don't want any of my furniture when I do move." Taylor said, "Cindy, all your things are brand new. Why don't you want them?" I said, "Because it's sitting in that house with the evil. The real reason I didn't want it was because I kept thinking if the evil could get into Lindsey, who's to say it couldn't get into the furniture and come out when ever it wanted." Taylor asked, "Then what are you going to do with everything? Sell it?" I said, "I guess so. I don't feel I have much choice." When Taylor and I hung up, Jake called and said that his dad took a turn for the worst and that he was in the intensive care unit. Jake wanted to know if I wanted to go up and see him. I said I wanted to. I hated to ask mom if she would watch the girls. She had already helped me out so much. Haley just happened to walk in. I told her about Jake's dad and she said that she would watch the girls. I said, "Thanks Haley, would you watch them at your house?" she asked me why she couldn't watch them at mom's house and I said, "Haley, you, me, and the girls have been staying here for a week and mom needs a break." Haley said, "How about I watch them at the spook house? That way they can play with Brett." I said, "Haley, you know Lindsey won't go up there." She said, "Ill talk her into it." While Haley was talking to Lindsey, I called Kendra and told her what was going on. She said she would be home, so if the girls wanted they could come stay with her. Haley said no that she would watch them. She said, "Well tell Haley that Brett can come over to play with the girls but if they get scared to come over to my place." I told Kendra thanks and I hung up the phone. I felt a lot better knowing that Kendra was going to be home. I don't know what Haley said to Lindsey but Lindsey was ready to go.

We all got in the van. Haley said that she wasn't scared because we had went up to do the wash so many times and nothing happened to her. When I got up the hill, I just didn't feel right about leaving them. Haley said, "We will be fine, just go." I stopped by Jake's and we were on our way to the hospital. I prayed for God to keep Haley and the girls safe. I prayed for Jake's dad also. Jake's dad was always good to me and my girls when Jake and I weren't together. I wondered if the evil had something to do with Jake's dads' illness. He had brought Jake up the day the police were there; he helped Jake move his things out of my house. Not long after that, he started getting sick. I said something to Jake about it. Jake said, "I don't know Cindy, dad was getting sick before we moved in, he just didn't go to the doctor."

Jake's mom and sisters were there. We took our turns going in to see him. We were there a few hours when Jake said he was going to call work and take off, his mom said, "No Jake, go in and if something should happen we will call your work." Jake was really upset when he left the hospital. I tried to comfort him, I really felt sorry for him. Half way home, Jake asked, "What's wrong?" I said, "Jake, I have a bad feeling something happened at the house." Jake said, "I'll ride with you to go and get Haley and the girls." It had been daylight when I dropped the girls off at the house, now it was dark. We were on our way up the hill when I noticed the house was dark. I said, "Oh, no I knew I shouldn't have left them alone." Kendra came running out of her trailer. I guess she knew by the look on my face that I was upset. She said, "Cindy everyone is ok." Then she began explaining what had happened. "Brett came over to play with girls. Haley took the kids into the TV room. She had some pens and paper. She was drawing pictures. She then said, "Ok kids lets make a book." The kids all said, "Yeah!" Haley said, "So what should we write about?" As soon as she asked that, the VCR came on by itself and it started rewinding. Kendra said Haley was the first one out the door; the kids followed her screaming and crying. Kendra let Haley use the phone to call mom to pick them up. Kendra said, "When your mom got here, Haley said that her purse was still in the house. Your mom said that she would go in with Haley to get it and Haley said that she wasn't going to go back in the house. Your mom had to go back in there by herself." I said, "Well mom gets sick every time she's in that house. I was told by the psychic for my mom not to come anywhere near the house." I took Jake home and I headed back to moms. When I walked in the girls started telling me what happened. Lindsey said, "Stupid Haley yelled all for one and one for all and then she left us." I looked at Haley and said, "I'm not scared, nothings going to happen." She said, Screw you Cindy! I didn't think anything would happen since you weren't in the house." I said, "Well, I didn't think it would either but then again, I had a feeling not to leave you guys up there. The main thing is that it didn't try to hurt anyone, it was just aggravating you guys. It wanted to scare you and it did."

Taylor called moms and said, "I know someone who will buy your bedroom set." I asked, "Who?" she said, "Me and Jesse." That was Taylor's latest boyfriend and she asked if they could come up and see it one day next week. I said, "Alright, I'll be at moms so give me a call." I told mom what Taylor had said. Mom said, " you will never get what you paid for it. Didn't Carrie tell you that the evil lives there and always has? if you sell everything, you will be sorry. You better think about this." I said, "I'll think about it mom."

I told Haley that we needed to start staying at her house a few nights. She said that if we did it, then it would have to be late before we go. I asked her why and she said that she was a couple of months behind on her rent. Haley had quit her job and with everything going on I didn't even think about her rent. Since the landlord lived right in front of her house, she was afraid to go home. So we waited until we thought they were in bed and we went to her house. That week I stayed all over, Jake's, Bridgets, Haleys, and moms. Taylor called mom to see if it was alright for her and Jesse to come look at the bedroom set. I said, "I guess so." She said, "Well what's wrong?" I said, "The last tour I gave of the house, one lady got a bloody lip. The psychic told me not to be taking people in the house. She said that someone was going to get hurt but I did it anyway." Taylor said, "All we want to do is look at the bedroom set." I said, "Ok." When they arrived at moms, we went over to the house. Everything seemed ok. When we got upstairs, Taylor was looking at the set and asked Jesse, "Do you like it?" He said, "Yes." It was a really nice set. I really hated selling it. I thought a lot about what mom said about selling everything I owned. I said to Taylor, "Well you saw it Taylor, let's go." Taylor said, "Wait a minute Cindy." She sat on the bed and started feeling the mattress. I started feeling nervous, I just wanted to leave. All at once Taylor stared screaming and flopping up and down on the bed. I panicked and ran for the stairs. Jesse said, "Cindy!" and I stopped. Then I heard Taylor laughing. I walked back to where they were. My heart was still beating out of my chest. I heard Jesse say, "Taylor, you almost gave me a heart attack. I don't think it was funny." Then he said, "I can't believe you would do that to your sister after everything she has been through." I looked at Taylor and said, "You're a bitch, I can't believe you would do that to me." She said, "I was just kidding with you guys." I said, "Come on, let's go." We went back to moms and they left.

    The next day I got a call from the realtor. She said, " they wouldn't give the people the loan but don't get upset because were working on another bank. They definitely want the house." I thought to myself, your working on it and the evil is working against it. After I got the call I was more depressed than I had been. That evening there a good movie on television; Mom made some popcorn for the girls. The girls were on the living room floor and I was stretched out on the couch. I felt mentally drained as I closed my eyes. I never meant to fall asleep but I did and the next thing I knew, I had left my body once again. I was still at mom's apartment but everything was different. The furniture in mom's room was different, all old fashioned. There were pictures on the walls of sunflowers and daisies. I walked into her kitchen and it to was also different. I can't really remember much about the kitchen but I do remember looking at the counter. There was an old fashioned coke bottle sitting there. I heard the TV playing and that's when I walked into the living room. I stood there looking at myself lying on the couch. With God as my witness, this is what I saw. There was a mass of energy moving around my body, I watched as it was trying to attack me. When it touched my body, the mid section of my body lit up like a cross. It reminded me of a bug zapper. The only time I could see the cross light up was when the energy tried to touch me. It was like the energy was being shocked. I was now back in my body and fully awake. I sat up and looked around the room. Everything was the same. Mom and the girls were still watching the movie. If everything else that happened to me sounded crazy, I knew that what I had just seen sounded unbelievable and the only eye witnesses were myself and God.

Jake and I had been arguing off and on like always. I had spoken to him the night before and he was supposed to meet me up at the house to do the wash. I didn't know where Haley was so I told mom that if she came by to tell her that I was up at the house doing wash. When I got to the house, Jake wasn't there. I stood outside for awhile and still no Jake. I walked into the house and called Jake's mom's house. She said he wasn't there and that he left over an hour ago. I told her that he was supposed to meet me to do the wash. She said that she didn't know where he was. When I hung up, I walked back outside. I stood there for awhile watching the cars passing from the hill. Jake wasn't one of them. The more I stood outside the more upset I got. I stood there thinking, "I own this house yet I'm afraid to even walk in by myself." I unleashed the dog and I walked in the house. I stood in the kitchen; I looked at the crucifix that was hanging on the kitchen wall. Maybe it was the combination of the crucifix and remembering the lighted cross that I had seen. I really don't know what possessed me to do what I did. Maybe it was the fact that I knew God was with me. I stood in the middle of the kitchen and yelled, "Alright you son of a bitch, you want this house, can have it. I didn't want it to begin with but you cant have me, I am a child of God and I belong to him. You have ruined my life and my children's life! I know that you have made the people I care about sick and probably half the town thinks I'm crazy! But that's what you wanted them to think, wasn't it?" I screamed and cursed the evil thing that had ripped my life apart. Then I said, "You can't hurt me anymore because I'm not afraid of you any longer!" Even though I said that, I was still afraid. I stood there waiting to take the beating that I was sure I was about to receive. I heard a car coming up the hill when I looked out the window, it was Haley. I ran outside, I was so glad to see her. I told her that Jake hadn't shown up. Haley helped me carry the clothes to the utility room. After the clothes started washing, we sat at the kitchen table and started talking. Haley didn't comment on how nervous I was. I guess she thought it was because Jake hadn't showed up earlier. If she would have known what I said moments before she drove up the hill, I doubt if she would have even came in the house. Haley walked into the utility room with me while I put the wet clothes in the dryer. When we got back to the kitchen, Haley said that she was hungry. She suggested a fast food place in Collinsville where we could order a taco salad to go then we could bring the food back and eat while the clothes were drying. When we got back from getting our taco salads, we went to the utility room to check the clothes, they were still damp. We went back to the kitchen table and started eating. All of the sudden I knew that we were no longer alone. I could feel someone watching us. I stopped eating and began looking around the kitchen. Haley asked, "What's wrong?" I replied, "Nothing Haley, nothing." Haley said, "Cindy, I know you, something is wrong and if you don't tell me right now then I'm leaving." I said, "Ok Haley. I did something stupid right before you drove up the hill." I proceeded to tell her what I did. Haley shook her head and said, "I'm getting the hell out of here!" I said, "No, don't leave me. If it was going to do something, it would have done it by now. I'm just nervous." Haley said, "Well those clothes better hurry up and dry." We checked the clothes and decided to take them out of the dryer even though all of them weren't dry. We took the clothes and went back up to mom's house.

A few days later, the house was to be shown again. Haley and I were in such a hurry to get out of there the day we went to do the wash that we left our Styrofoam boxes that our taco salads came in on the kitchen table. That meant that I would have to go back up to the house and clean off the table. I said something to Sydney about having to go up to the house and as always, she offered to go with me. We went to the house and I straighten my mess up in about a minute and we were out of there. A few days later, the realtor called again and said the loan didn't go through but they were going to try one more bank. After I hung up, Haley said that her landlord said she had to get her belongings out of her house. I said, "Well, that's just great Haley, now what are you going to do?" she said, "I guess I'll store some of my things and stay here." I said, "Haley, moms going to have a fit. I know she loves all of us but this is too much on her. I am about ready to go home myself, I'm tired of running. Haley, do you realize that I have been staying here at moms, your house, Jake's mom's basement, and Bridgets and Dougs. I'm surprised the girls are still making good grades. I'm tired of being homeless, besides I miss all my possessions. We all need some stability in our lives, something we haven't had in a long time." Haley agreed to move in the house with us. I spoke to the girls about the situation. I knew Sydney would agree with whatever I decided but I wasn't sure about Lindsey. Lindsey said she would stay at my moms that she was not staying at the house. The way I saw it, one person staying with mom would be a lot easier. After all, it would only be until the house sold. I called Kendra and told her that we were moving back home. She was really happy. Brett had walked over to moms a few times to see the girls so he would be happy to know that Sydney was moving back home. Although everyone we stayed with more than welcomed us, I was glad to be going home, home to the place that I had been running from all these months. It seemed strange to me that I even wanted to go back. The one thing I wouldn't do in the house was go to sleep. I already knew I could go months without sleeping so that shouldn't be a problem. I was hoping that it wouldn't take months for the house to sell.

Sydney agreed to go with me to take the first load of our things from moms to the house. Lindsey was going to ride with Haley to get some of her possessions out of her house and she would meet us back at moms. We had just driven up the hill when Kendra greeted us. I told her we were taking some of our stuff in and that we would be back with the rest of our things. When got back to moms, I pulled around to the back parking lot when a yellow van blocked me in. I looked at Sydney and asked, "Who is he? What does he think he's doing?" He knew I wanted by but he wouldn't move. I hit the lock button on my door which locked all the doors in my van. I finally pushed the button to roll down my window. He looked at me and said, "I know what's going on with you." I said, "Excuse me?" He then said, "I know why these things are happening in your house." I asked, "Who are you?" he said his name was Steven. I asked him how he knew I was here. He said that someone told him where to find me. He started telling me things about the area where my mom lives; Things that took place before I was born. I heard the same stories from people who had lived here all their lives, I knew just about everybody in Caseyville, if not by name then by face. This man I had never seen before. He looked to be in his early forties. He said, "Make sure and tell your mom to be careful of a fire because her house isn't really wired very well." He started talking about my house. He told me that the evil wants me to sacrifice myself. I said, "Well there's no way I'm going to do that." Sydney said, "Mom, I'm scared." I was getting a little scared myself. Sydney and I both noticed he had what looked like blood on his forehead. He said something about a little boy and a little girl. One of them was killed trying to protect the other from their father. He asked, "Did you see a little boy in the house?" I said, "Yes." He asked if I saw the little girl. I told him no. He said, "Well go to the library." He gave me a day and year, I can't remember now if it was 1932 or 1934. The month was March. He said, "The answer to what's going on is in the newspaper." Then he asked if my girls had been physically hurt. I said, "Mainly it liked to scare them although it did hold Sydney up so she couldn't move." He said, "Let me go in the house and sacrifice myself then it will not bother you or your girls ever again." I didn't know this man or what he had been on but I just wanted to get away from him. He was still sitting in his van and I was sitting in mine. He kept saying, "Come on, and take me to the house." He said, "You can even call your mom's landlord, he knows me." I said, "Ok, I'll be right back." I looked at Sydney and told her to get out of the van and start running down to grandmas. I said, "I'm getting out also Sydney." We both ran to moms. When we walked in moms she said, "I've been watching out the window, who is blocking your van?" I explained as quickly as I could what the man had said. I looked out the window and he was gone. We walked outside and there was no sign of him anywhere. We looked up and down the street. He was nowhere in sight. It was as if he disappeared into thin air. I called my mom's landlord and he said that his nephew had hung around a boy named Steve but that had been many years ago. His nephew had drowned and the boy had moved away and they had never heard from him again. I went to the police station and told them how the man had blocked me in mom's house and what he had said. I gave them a description of the man and his van. I then went back to mom's house. Sydney went with me to the police station and on the way home she said, "Mom, I don't think we should go back to the house to stay." I said, "I don't either Sydney. I'm afraid the man will come to the house." When I got to moms, I said, "Mom, I'm too afraid to go back home, maybe this Steven came to your house for a reason. Maybe I wasn't supposed to go back." I called Kendra and told her what had happened with the man. She said that she would go up to the library with me and look up the date he gave me in the newspaper. We decided we would go as soon as the kids were in school Monday morning. I don't know who was more excited to find out what the newspaper had to say, me or Kendra. It was Saturday so I had another day to wait. Monday morning finally arrived. After our kids were on the school bus, Kendra and I met and headed up to Belleville library which was one of the largest libraries in our area. When we walked in, it was packed. There were a lot of students there. We spoke to the librarian and told her we needed to see a newspaper and gave her the month, day, and year. She told us that it was on micro film. She helped us find what we were looking for. The film was dated from the beginning of the month. We had the film in our hands, next we had to wait for the machine. Everyone and their brother were looking up micro film so we had to wait our turn. It took us a few hours but it was finally our turn. We put the film in and began searching for the day the man had told me to look up. The film went to Friday to Sunday. The day we were looking for was Saturday. Kendra and I both looked at one another and said, "What the hell is going on?" We backed the film up and looked again. Saturday was missing. I went and got the librarian and asked her where Saturday was. She said that it was odd that it should have been there. Even the librarian couldn't understand what was going on. I looked at Kendra and she said, "Cindy this is really weird" I said, "yeah Kendra, I know, I guess I'm not supposed to find out what happened in that house years ago." Kendra was just as disappointed as I was. We had spent hours at the library and for what? We still didn't know any more than we did before we came to Belleville. Only God knows for sure what took place on that land and in the house so many years ago. When I got back to moms, Jake called. He said, "Cindy, I have solved all our problems." He explained that he had found a trailer that someone was selling real cheap. I said, "Jake, you know how I feel about trailers." A friend of mine had burnt up in a trailer and I was always afraid of them every since. That was back when I was a teenager and the truth was, I hated everything he had put me through. Jake insisted that I look at the trailer. He came by and picked me up. When he started driving out of Caseyville I asked where the trailer was located. He said, "You'll see, it's not very far." When we were out of Collinsville, I wondered how much further it was. I said, "Jake, wherever this trailer is, did you even check about the school district?" He said, "No, not yet." We were on our way to Granite City when we turned into a nice trailer park and it even had a lake there. He kept driving until we came to a trailer with a screened in front porch, the trailer looked pretty nice. I was surprised that Jake had a key. The inside looked alright but it was really dirty. Jake asked how I liked it. I said, "Its nice Jake, at least it would be if it was cleaned up." Jake said, "Well , you don't have to run from place to place any longer because I bought the trailer." He hadn't even talked it over with me first, he bought it and assumed I would like it and move right in. When it came to me, Jake was always so sure of himself. Jake dropped me off at moms and I told her about the trailer. She asked me what we were going to do when the house sold. I said, "Jake said he would turn around and sell the trailer because he could get more out of it then what he paid for it." Mom knew I wasn't too keen on trailers to begin with. I decided I would just drive the girls back in forth to school, they had already been through enough already. I wasn't going to pull them out of school and put them into another one where they didn't know anyone.

 That weekend, Jake and I took girls over to the trailer. I swept the floors and started cleaning the trailer when I went to get some water in a bucket. I noticed the water seemed rusty. I said, "Jake come look at this water." He said that the trailer had been sitting awhile so the water hadn't been running through the pipes in a long time. I believed him, I didn't know any better. I found out that the toilet wouldn't flush either. He said he would have the toilet fixed by tomorrow. After I cleaned everything up, the kids and I went back to moms, we were supposed to move our stuff in Sunday. I told Haley that I didn't want to stay by myself at night in a strange place. She said she would stay there with me when Jake was at work.

I drove Haley over to show her where the trailer was. The girls and I started moving our stuff in Sunday morning. When it was time for us to take a bath, the tub was filled with nasty, rusty water. I had to load the girls up and take them back to moms to get a bath. When we got back to the trailer, I went in the kitchen to make me some tea and I got the same rusty water. There was no store close by so we went into Collinsville to get soda. Haley arrived that evening and I told her that we couldn't use the water or flush the toilet. Leave it to Jake, all he wanted was a bed.

I was sick of running back and forth and not having any water. The girls were already sleeping but I decided this would be our last night in the trailer. It still didn't seem clean to me. I mopped with dirty, rusty water. I should have never agreed to stay there to begin with. The next morning when Jake came home, I got the girls up for school and told Jake I would be back after I took them to school. I stopped by moms and asked if me and the girls could move back in. She said, "Sure." I was relived. I had been using a lot of gas running the girls to and from school, plus to moms at night for baths. I went back to Jakes and let him know we werent going to be staying there any longer. I started gathering up mine and the girls' belongings. He said, "Your not going anywhere!" I said, "Watch me!" He grabbed a hold of my arm. I said, "Let go now Jake or ill get the police to get our things!" he said, "If it weren't for you, I would have never bought this trailer." I said, "Jake, you didn't even ask me to begin with. You took it upon yourself without even consulting me first. Damn Jake, you can't even use the water in this place or flush the toilet. Do you really think this place is sanitary? Some of the floors are even falling through. You didn't show me this place before you bought it because you knew that I would have said no. All the pipes are busted in this dump and I know you knew it before you bought it. So don't you dare blame me for you buying this dump! Besides it's about time you got your own place."

I took one load to moms and went back for the second load. Thank God l hadn't let Jake talk me into bringing any of my furniture over. He had went to the house and got a lot of toys; now I had to haul them all back. When I came back for the second load, I noticed my radio and a few other things were missing. I asked Jake where my things were and he said that he didn't know. I said, "That's ok Jake, I guess you need them worse than me and the kids do." By the time I got back to moms, I was worn out. I was sitting there feeling sorry myself when the phone rang, it was Bridget. I told her what had happened with me and Jake. She said, "Well maybe the house will get sold soon." I said that I was still waiting to find out if the people that were interested got the loan. When we hung up, Allie called me. She wanted to know if I would let her aunt Donna come up to the house. She had a lot of psychic ability. I ask Allie if her aunt knew what she was walking in to. Wasn't she afraid? She said, no, that she had been in haunted houses before but nothing like mine. Allie said, "Cindy, she is very religious. She said that she would pray before she went in the house and after she came out." I told Allie to call me back and let me know when she wanted to come over.

 I went to pick the girls up from school. I explained that we would be staying at grandmas again for awhile. They seemed relieved. They were also tired of the nasty trailer and running back and forth. The girls said that they were invited to a slumber party and they needed to get their sleeping bags at the house. This was one thing Sydney and I didn't want to do. The sleeping bags were in the bedroom closet upstairs in what use to be the girls bedroom. I called Allie back and told her about the sleeping bags. I said, "Tell your Aunt Donna if she wants to see the house that I would take her up within the next few days because I have to have the sleeping bags by the following weekend." Her aunt agreed to come whenever I wanted her to. So we set a day and a time I was to meet her at Katlin's house. The day arrived and I went to Katlins and met Donna. Allie was there and so was Donna's son Sam. Sam was young; he looked to be around seventeen years old. When it was time for us to go I said, "Why don't you come with us Allie? You too Katlin." They both declined. Donna, Sam, and I rode up to the house. Donna prayed before we even entered the house, which made me feel a lot better. Once in the house, we walked around downstairs then we went upstairs. When we got to the girls' room I said, "Donna, what ever you do, please don't leave me in here." She assured me that she wasn't going to leave me. I opened the closet door and bent over looking for the sleeping bags. They should have been right there but they weren't. I thought they would be. I had a weird feeling. I knew something was there besides us. I turned my head back out of the closet and was shocked to find Donna gone. I panicked and started yelling her name. I saw her standing in the living room with her back towards me. I ran in the living room and stood in front of her. I was really upset. I asked her why she had left me. She said, "I thought Sam was smoking a cigarette." I thought to myself, "What the hell did Sam's smoking a cigarette have to do with leaving me? It didn't make sense because Sam smoked right in front of her. We walked downstairs. I still didn't have the sleeping bags at this point, I didn't care any longer, I just wanted to leave. We were in the Kitchen when Donna and Sam were talking to each other about something they had smelled. Donna said, "It's following Cindy." I thought, oh no not again. Donna said, "Smell it Cindy, Its right by you." I was shocked. Instead of the rotten smell, this smelled like roses. Donna said, " you have a good spirit in this house also." When we left, Donna prayed again.

When we got back to Katlin's house, Donna turned to me and said, " I'm sorry I left you in the bedroom. Now I will tell you the truth. While you were looking in the closet, a blast of cold air came out and went right through me. It was so strong that I almost passed out. I didn't want to faint in front of you so I walked into the next room." She then said, "Feel your pants and then feel mine." Donna's pants were still as cold as ice. Allie and Katlin felt them also and they were shocked. Allie called me a few days later and wanted to go up to the house. I was really surprised; she would never come up before. She came over to mom's house and we drove up the hill to the house. We were upstairs and I was telling Allie that I needed to keep all the furniture except I knew I would have to sell one of my living room sets. I knew wherever I ended up; .I wouldn't have two living rooms again. She told me to let her know which one I wanted to sell because she wanted to buy one. All the sudden, Allie jumped and said, "Cindy, something just stuck me!" I said, "Don't worry about it, I get stuck and burned all the time, it wont leave a mark." She said, "Come on Cindy, lets get the hell out of here!"

I was sitting there at moms one day when the phone rang. It was Bridget and she asked if I had sold the house yet. I told her no that I was still waiting to hear something. She said, "Cindy, I can get you a double wide trailer fairly cheap. I said, "Forget it! I don't want a trailer." She said, "Just let me take you to look at it and you will change your mind." I said, "Bridget, I hate trailers." She said, "It's beautiful, it's more like a house than a trailer. Trust me; you'll love it when you see it. It's not even that far away, it's in Caseyville close to where Haley lives." I said, "I don't know." She said that she was coming up to moms. When we hung up, I told mom what Bridget had said. She said, " you can at least look at it." When Bridget came over to moms, I agreed to look at the trailer. I told her I doubted if I would like it. When we got up to the trailer park, Bridget pulled up to a double wide trailer. It looked really nice on the outside; it even had a bay window. She put the key in the lock and turned the knob on the door. When we walked in it looked more like a house on the inside than a trailer. It was very nice but there were some things that were wrong. Someone had broken in and striped the trailer of the light fixtures and ceiling fans, they even took the central air unit. It still was a beautiful trailer. The carpets were dirty and so were the rooms. I would have a lot of cleaning to do but I knew it was well worth it. I looked around the kitchen, it was filthy as well. The kitchen counters were really dirty. I looked at Bridget and said, "I love it! It needs a good cleaning but other than that, it's beautiful." I told Bridget I was going to try to get the money up. I knew it was going to be hard keeping the mortgage up on the house plus paying lot rent but somehow I knew I would do it. I wasn't about to give up now, I had come this far. Besides, God had never let me down before and I knew he wouldn't let me down now. With his help, I knew everything would somehow work out. I had been praying asking God to help me find a way out of this mess that me and the girls were in. To me, this was the answer to my prayers.

 I made a few phone calls and was told that I could get the money in a few days. I went to Bridget's and told her I would have the money by the weekend. She handed me the key and said I could go on in and start cleaning it up. Bridget spoke to the manager of the trailer park. I was to go to the office and fill out an application. The previous owners owed back lot rent that was to be paid. I also had to pay two months rent in advance. The previous owners also left behind a big water bill that had to be paid. Since I had no water or electricity yet, I took a broom over to the trailer and swept it out. I took cleaner and cleaned the counters and wiped all the glass cabinets. I worked for hours and the place started shaping up. I went back to moms and called about getting the gas and electric turned on. Then I went to the water department and asked them to turn the water on in my name. I went by my house and feed the dog because Jake hadn't been up to feed her. I grabbed my big cooler and a lamp from the house. When I went back to the trailer, I waited for the water to be turned on and I prayed that the pipes wouldn't be busted. After all, the trailer had sat all winter long. My prayers were answered once again when the water was turned on and the pipes weren't busted. I said, "thank you God." By the time the girls and I were ready to move in, the place was spotless. I had even cleaned every wall. The girls helped out a lot after school.

 It was Saturday morning when I planned for the girls and I to spend the night in the trailer. We had spent the night at moms Friday night so we got up early Saturday morning. Sydney and I went up to the house and grabbed some toys and a few other things. When we got to the trailer, I looked at the living room curtains and they were filthy. I said, "Well Sydney, those drapes have to come down." There were two pairs. I said, "what I'm going to do is take them to the house and wash them in the bathtub then take them downstairs and put them in the washer. She said, "Ok mom, I'll go with you." Since my washer and dryer along with everything else were at the house, I didn't have any choice. I went by mom's house and told her and Lindsey what we were going to do. While I was at moms, I phoned Kendra and told her about the trailer. She said, "I can't believe it, I know right where your trailer is at. Brett's new babysitter lives right next door." She said that his babysitter's name was Amy. She said, "She has a girl your girls' age and two sons." She told me that if anything should happen at the house, she would call Amy and give her a message to give me. I told her that my phone service would be on Monday, and then I would call her and give her my new number. When I hung up, I told mom that I would be back to get Lindsey as soon as the drapes were through.

We headed over to the house. I was so happy about moving into the trailer that I wasn't scared when I walked into the house. I put the first set of drapes in the bath tub and started scrubbing them out and letting them drain. I said, "Sydney, I'm going to go in my bedroom and get a pair of jeans out of my closet." When I got into the living room, I looked around. Everything seemed just fine. Mom had got each of my girl's old fashioned dolls a few years ago. The dolls each held an umbrella in their hand. I noticed one of the dolls were standing on the living room TV, someone must have put it there. I didn't think anything about it. I went in the bedroom and got my jeans. Sydney was right on my heels as always. We went back into the bathroom and I took the drapes out of the tub and took them downstairs and put them into the washer. I said, "Well Sydney, one set left to go." We climbed back up the stairs. I put the rest of the drapes in the tub and began scrubbing. All at once the bathroom door slammed. I jumped and turned around. Sydney had a frightened look on her face. She was standing in front of the door blocking it. I asked, "What do you think your doing Sydney?" I felt safer with the door open. That way if anything happened, we could run straight down the stairs. I said, "Sydney, open the door now!" Sydney wouldn't say anything at first; she just kept staring at me. I said again, "Open the door Sydney!" She said, "please mom, don't open the door. The doll on the TV is looking at us." I said, "She can't be. I noticed her when I went to get jeans, she was facing the fireplace." Sydney said, "Well she's not now mom, I swear." I said, "damn it Sydney, Move!" I opened the door and said, "Look!" I let out a scream because the doll was indeed starting at us. I grabbed Sydney's hand and we ran down the steps and outside. I tried to calm down. I paced back and forth praying. I looked over at Kendra's but her car was gone. I said, "Sydney, I have to go back in the house. We can't stay in the trailer tonight without something to cover up the windows, anyone could look at us. Sydney why don't you stay here and I'll run up the stairs real fast and finish the drapes. She said, "No mom, I'll go with you."

We stayed outside a good fifteen minutes. We walked back inside; I tried to get the light around us like the one Carrie had taught me. I hurried up and got the drapes done. I took the ones that were drying out and hung them on the line outside. It was March and it was still cold out. While I hung those, I had the others rinsing. When they were through, I put them in the dryer and took off. Sydney and I went back to moms. We told her what had happened. We stayed at moms for a few hours. I told mom I was going to go back and get the drapes then head back to the trailer. Lindsey threw a fit. She wanted me to go get the drapes then come back and get her. I said, "No." I told her Sydney would sit in the van while I got the drapes. When we got ready to leave, mom hugged me and told me to be careful. I said that I would and that I was going to run in the house and get the drapes and come right back out. When we got up the hill, Sydney was worried about me going in the house by myself. I told her I would be ok. I said, "Just take care of Lindsey." Lindsey was crying because she didn't want to be anywhere near the house. I got out of the van and took the drapes off the clothesline and put them in the van. Sydney asked, "Are you afraid to go in the house by yourself?" I said, "No Sydney, I'll be ok." The truth be known, I didn't want to go back in the house but I pretended I wasn't afraid. I looked at the girls and said; "I'll be right back." Everything seemed fine when I walked into the house. It looked as normal as anyone else's house. It was nice and quiet until I walked into the utility room. I bent down to get the drapes out of the dryer when I heard voices all around me. They were so loud. I covered my ears for a moment. I got the drapes out of the dryer and stood up. The voices were all around me, I heard male voices as well as female voices. I couldn't understand what they were saying. Their words all ran together. I could feel the spirits as well as hear them. I knew I had to get out of there. I prayed, "Jesus son of God, have mercy on me." I said, "God please help me! God is stronger than evil." I had the drapes in my arms. I pushed my shoulders together and bent down running through the spirits. When I got outside, I jumped in the van and drove off like a mad woman.

When we got to the trailer, I put the drapes up. The ones that were on the line were still damp but I didn't care. They were clean and no one could look in at us. I was sitting on the floor thinking about the voices I had heard. I thanked God for helping me get out of that house. The girls and I sat in the middle of the living room floor. I prayed over and over not to let the evil find us. I looked around the room. Even though it was empty, I wouldn't have been any happier if I would have been sitting in a mansion full of furniture. This trailer was ours, a place we could call home, we were no longer homeless. As long as the evil remained at the house, I knew that we would be alright. My biggest fear was the evil following us. The girls and I were sitting there in the quiet when we heard a strange howling noise. We all looked at one another. I finally figured out that it was just the March winds. It was getting late. I had the bible open when I heard a knock at the door, it was a woman. She asked, "Cindy?" I said, "Yes." She said, "I'm Amy, Kendra's friend." I said, "Hi." She said, "Kendra just called and said a bunch of young guys are up at your house. She told them she was going to call the police and they said to call you because they were friends of your uncle's Girlfriend Jennifer. Anyway Kendra is holding them up there until you come see what's going on." I said, "Jennifer lives in the double wide behind you Amy. Would you call Kendra back and tell her I'm on my way?" Both of the girls said, "Mom, I don't want to go." I said, "Look you two, Kendra is going to have those guys arrested if we don't go up there. If they know Jennifer then they are curious about the house and I don't want them to go to jail. Now come on!" it was late and I didn't want to go up that hill anymore than my daughters did but I couldn't see some innocent guys going to jail for trespassing either. When we reached the hill, both of my daughters said, "Mom, please don't make us go in the house." Kendra's boyfriend Bruce was there and said that the girls could stay in their trailer until I got finished talking to the guys. I walked over to where the guys were. They said they were sorry that one of the boys' mom worked with Jennifer at the bank and he had heard so much about the house that he wanted to see it. He had told his friends and they decided to come up and look at it. I explained that the girls and I were staying at our new trailer and that it was our first night there. The one guy asked since I was already there if I would give them a tour of the house. I said, "I don't know. I had a really bad experience in the house earlier today. I don't really want to go back in there tonight." I explained about the doll and the voices. I looked at their faces, I could tell they were disappointed because I wouldn't take them in the house. I stood there for a minute thinking that the boys had went through enough already. They weren't from this area and they had a hard time finding the place plus Kendra had scared them when she said she was calling the police and wouldn't let them leave. I said, "I'll go ahead and take you guys in and give you a tour of the house. It's going to be a quick one though. I'm going to walk over to Kendras and tell her what is going on in case something would happen." When I came back, I unlocked the door and we walked in, I gave them a tour of the house. One of the guys said something about all my furniture. I said, "Everything I own is in this house, that's why Kendra keeps such a close eye on it." One of them asked if we had anything in the tralier yet. I said, "No, As a matter of fact, the girls and I were sitting in an empty trailer when a neighbor came over to tell me Kendra called about you guys. I don't even have my phone service turned on yet." The guys looked at one another and said, "We have a couple of trucks parked right outside, their small but they can hold pretty much. How about we move some of this furniture into your trailer for you and your girls?" I said, "You guys don't have to do this you know." They said, "We know, we just want to help you." I felt like crying. I had spoken to Jake on the phone the previous day and told him that I had bought a double wide trailer and that I needed help moving our things but he didn't offer to help. Bridget and Doug had a truck but they had already done so much for me that I didn't want to bother them. All my men friends I had, Jake had chased off years ago. I really had no idea how I was ever going to get the furniture out of the house. It was strange, before Amy came over me and the girls had been sitting in the middle of the living room floor and I had thought to myself that I wished that the girls had their beds at the trailer or at least the couch in the TV room because it made out into a bed. Now these guys were going to move our furniture in for us. I asked the guys if they were sure they wanted to do this. They said, "You were nice enough to bring us in the house, besides we don't have anything better to do." I knew they had better things to do. They were young and this was the weekend. They went into the TV room and picked up the couch. It was really heavy because it had a bed built in it. One of the guys said, "Put it down!" When the couch was down the guy ran out to the porch. I noticed a trail of blood from the couch to where he was standing. I asked, "are you ok?" he said that it felt like someone stuck him with something sharp. We went in and checked the couch but we couldn't find anything. I had never seen so much blood come out of a small prick on the finger. As quickly as the blood poured out, it stopped. I said, "Look guys, you don't have to move any of this furniture. Its ok, ill find some way to get it moved." They said, "No." and they continued moving the furniture to the trucks. I told them to get what they could in the trucks then lock the door. I went to Kendras and got the girls. By the time the trucks were loaded up, we were ready to go. I didn't really pay attention to what they had in the trucks, it was dark out and I just wanted away from the house. I turned the van around and they followed me down the hill. When we got to my trailer, I unlocked the door and the guys started unloading the trucks. I couldn't believe how much furniture they had brought. They had my living room set that was in the TV room, my kitchen set, the girls' bunk beds, and my microwave cart among other things. They even put the kids' bunk beds together. I was so grateful for all that they had done for me and the girls. These were all good looking guys and I'm sure that they all had girlfriends yet they took their time to make sure the girls and I had a bed to sleep in and a couch to sit on.

When they left, I thanked God for bringing the guys to my house. I asked God to bless them, protect them and watch over them. I knew these guys were very special and I knew that I would never forget what they did for me and the girls. When the guys had left, Sydney and Lindsey walked over to where I was sitting. They both asked why I was crying. I said, "Its not because I'm sad." Sydney asked, "Is it because the boys were so nice mom." the way they helped you?" I said, "Yes." For once these were tears of joy. I told my girls, "I do believe everything will work out for us now." I went to moms the next day and told her about the guys moving most of the furniture. She was really happy for me. I called Allie and told her about it and she was happy for me too. Allie decided she wanted to buy the other living room set that was in the living room upstairs. When she brought her husband by to look at the set, they decided to move my bedroom set, refrigerator, stove, and my washer and dryer. Jake came by the house to get the dog so he ended helping Allie's husband with my things. Allie started picking up the large bags that I had filled with clothes. She put some in the back of the truck. Allie had a truck and so did her husband. Both trucks were packed and most of my things were out of the house. I was real thankful to have a friend like Allie. Allie and her husband paid me for the living room set and took it to their home. I decided I would go back and get what was left in the next few days. I wanted to get back to the trailer and get everything put away. When I was through hanging pictures and had everything in place, the trailer really looked like home. It took me two days to get everything organized. I went back up to the house and gave it a good cleaning. When I was through, I was exhausted so I decided I would come back in the morning and get the last load. The next morning, I took the girls to school and headed for the house. I prayed before I went in as I always did. I put the key in the lock and turned the knob. Nothing could prepare me for what I saw. I walked into the kitchen and my kitchen ceiling was on the floor. I remember screaming, "No. no, no!" The floor was soak and wet and plaster was all over the floor. Thank God the real estate people got me insurance. I stood there looking around, it was such a mess. The realtor couldn't show the house like this. I went to moms and explained what happened and I called the realtor. I told them about the ceiling and how I would get it fixed as soon as I could. I said when it was repaired; I would give them a call.

I called several places and I couldn't believe the amount they were asking just to come out and look at it. I was in tears when I called Kendra to see if she knew anyone in that line of work. Kendra knew a lot of people.

Kendra said, "My brother does that type of work. I'll try to get a hold of him and I'll get back to you." I went back to the house and cleaned up the mess. A few days later, Kendra's brother met me up at the house. He told me to go upstairs and fill the bathtub with water. I did then he said, "Let the water out." Next, he told me to flush the toilet. And then he told me to fill the sink and then let the water out. Then it was back to the bathtub. This went on and on. I was tired of running up and down the stairs. Finally he said, "Cindy, I don't understand what's going on here. There are no leaks and no busted pipes. There is no logical explanation for this." Evidently he didn't know what had been going on in the house. He didn't understand but I did. It was another way for the evil to keep me coming to the house. I looked at Kendra's brother and said, "Just fix the ceiling." He got the materials he needed and got the ceiling fixed. When I walked into the kitchen and looked up at the ceiling, I couldn't tell anything had been wrong with it. It was just like the rest of the house, it looked so normal and yet I knew the truth, it was possessed by evil. Even after I moved into the trailer, it took me months before I would even drive past the house. I would always take the long way when I would go to visit my mom. I finally got brave enough to start driving past the house.

One day I had been visiting my mom and was on my way home I saw my Uncle Tim; he lived next door to moms. When I drove by, Uncle Todd was standing outside in Tim's driveway. As I was driving by, Tim motioned for me to come back. I turned my van around and drove back. I got out of my van and Todd asked how I was doing. I answered him by saying, "I'm doing a lot better now." I told him that I was trying to forget what happened but I don't think I'll ever really forget it. Todd said,"Cindy, I just wanted to let you know that I'm very proud of you. You're a lot stronger than I had realized. Anyone else would have cracked under the circumstances." I said, "Todd, there were times when I didn't think I could go on. It was really hard. If I wouldn't have had family and friends standing by me, I don't know what would have happened." We talked a few more minutes then I got in my van and drove off. I put my Michael McDonald tape on. I was listening to a song called "No Looking Back" it seemed like the appropriate song after all I had gone through. I slowed down when I got by my house. I parked on the street. I just sat there staring at the house on the hill. I sat there thinking God is stronger than evil. As many times as I said it, I never knew the real meaning until now. I just realized what Father Anderson and my grandma had been trying to tell me. God is stronger than evil. I know he is; I am living proof. I cranked the volume up on my tape player and as I pushed on the gas pedal and drove away, I felt better than I had in a long time. The house finally sold in the fall of 1992.

As I come to the end of my story, I remember something one of my cousins had said when he was very young. He had been playing outside when he saw some construction workers digging. He went over to them and said, "Don't dig too deep, you might let the devil out." At the time we all thought it was funny and we laughed. Now I remember Father Anderson asking if we had disturbed anything at the house when we moved in. As I sit here, I think about when we first moved in the house, I can remember how Jake and I dug and dug to get all the roots out of the ground. Now I wonder if Jake and I dug just a little too deep.

Jake and I parted company but we still keep in touch.

Kendra and Brett moved off the hill shortly after I sold the house. Kendra and I remain good friends.

Aunt Joy came to me in a dream. She said I was going to have another baby. When I awoke, I thought the dream was crazy since I couldn't have anymore children. I called my Mom and told her about what Aunt Joy had said. A month later, I woke up with what I thought was the flu. Aunt Joy was right. On September 4th, 1993, I gave birth to a 6 pound 7 ounce baby girl. I would like to say our lives are perfect now but that would be a lie. Sydney, Lindsey, and I, still have horrible nightmares about the house and the evil. I pray every night for the light to be around my family. I wish there were someway I could erase from our memories the hell we went through but I know that's impossible. What happened to us, is something we will never forget. We sleep with our bedroom lights on and my bible is always opened to Psalms 91".

Made in the USA
Coppell, TX
03 August 2024

35536168R00069